ONE GUILTY MAN

A Courtroom Drama & Crime Thriller

Derik Brandt

DERIK BRANDT

Copyright © 2024 Derik Brandt

All rights reserved.

The characters and events portrayed in this book are fictitious. Any similarity to real persons, living or dead, is coincidental and not intended by the author.

No part of this book may be reproduced, or stored in a retrieval system, or transmitted in any form or by any means, electronic, mechanical, photocopying, recording, or otherwise, without express written permission of the publisher.

ISBN: 978-1-0688985-1-8

*This book is dedicated to my late father,
Heinz Brandt.*

CONTENTS

Title Page

Copyright

Dedication

CHAPTER 1	1
CHAPTER 2	4
CHAPTER 3	17
CHAPTER 4	24
CHAPTER 5	31
CHAPTER 6	40
CHAPTER 7	52
CHAPTER 8	63
CHAPTER 9	66
CHAPTER 10	77
CHAPTER 11	84
CHAPTER 12	100
CHAPTER 13	118
CHAPTER 14	125

CHAPTER 15   131

About The Author   137

CHAPTER 1

The Envelope

Robert's fingers grazed the envelope he plucked from his mailbox, his heart quickening at the sight of the jury duty summons. Fetching the mail had always been a routine chore, but today it felt different, almost momentous. The crisp, white envelope stood out against the usual bills and flyers, bringing an unexpected tension to his carefully ordered life.

In the serene tranquility of his front yard, amidst the familiar symphony of suburban sounds, Robert experienced a whirlwind of emotions. A retired cop with an unblemished record, yet concealing the truth of a murder committed in the shadows of his new life. The envelope felt heavier than mere paper, bearing the weight of his guilt and the burden of his secrets.

As Robert's eyes scanned the envelope, a

familiar scene unfolded at the edge of his vision: his white German Shepherd tentatively approaching the neighbor's black cat who, as she often did, had ventured into their yard. Each cautious step forward of the Shepherd was met with a swipe of the cat's paw, a ballet of feline grace and canine playfulness. The dog persisted in its attempts to forge a new friendship, undeterred by the cat's dismissive, if not even aggressive, gestures.

This cat had learned through experience that dogs were not to be trusted. Despite their outward appearance of friendliness, dogs were nothing more than big, drooling animals in the eyes of this cat. Their unpredictable behavior made them potentially dangerous which was enough to make any feline wary.

With a hesitant sigh, Robert tore open the envelope, the sound shattering the tranquility of the yard like a thunderclap. He glanced around anxiously, half-expecting the neighbors to emerge and demand an explanation from him. Satisfied that he was alone, he retreated indoors after calling his dog, who was now eager to be with someone who was already a friend.

As Robert perused the official summons, the bold text blurred before his eyes, the weight of his conflicting emotions bearing down upon him. Was this a call to serve justice or a reckoning for his own sins? The lie at the core of his existence tugged at him, mocking his beliefs and challenging his sense of self. How could he stand in judgment of another when his own guilt loomed over him like a specter in the night?

CHAPTER 2

Voir Dire

Three weeks had passed since Robert received the summons for jury duty. Now here he sat, in the lobby of the courthouse. The lobby was a cavernous space with marble floors that echoed every footstep. Large windows allowed beams of sunlight to filter through. There were a few scattered benches where it seemed other potential jurors were sitting, fidgeting with their phones or flipping through magazines. The walls were adorned with solemn portraits of past judges, their stern expressions adding to the weight of the place. Some of the portraits seemed so similar to each other that Robert couldn't always tell if the different portraits weren't actually of the same judge. And almost all seem to be standing in front of an American flag. But then Robert's thoughts raced back to the matters at hand. Those three weeks had seemed like an eternity to Robert, the anticipation and dread building with each passing day.

After a brief wait in the lobby, he and four others were called into the courtroom for the jury selection process. The courtroom was an imposing chamber with high ceilings, polished wooden pews, and a judge's bench that stood elevated, symbolizing the authority of the judicial system. The air was thick with the scent of aged wood. Robert sat in the jury box with the others, his eyes wandering over the room's somber decor — the American flag standing tall in one corner, the state seal prominently displayed behind the judge's bench.

The judge, a grizzled man with a stern face and a mane of white hair, presided over the room with an air of unwavering authority. His voice echoed through the courtroom, each word striking Robert like a hammer on his conscience. He felt as though he displayed signs of physical pain that everyone must have noticed. But Robert had only barely begun to feel the weight of his conscience as the judge continued to speak. Hit by a hammer? Who cares? A hammer's blow is localized, the consequences generally straightforward and predictable, and certainly within the realm of Robert's life experiences. No, what Robert was about to learn would hit him like a wrecking ball!

Robert's heart nearly stopped when the judge announced the case details. The defendant, a weary-looking man in his thirties, sat slumped at the defense table, his eyes hollow and his hands nervously twisting a handkerchief. His face bore the lines of someone who had seen too much hardship, and his clothes, though neat, hung loosely on his gaunt frame. He looked like a man who had been worn down by life, and now, the weight of the murder charge seemed to crush him further.

The judge began to describe the case, and Robert's blood ran cold as the details unfolded. The crime had occurred two years ago, and the specifics were chillingly familiar. The victim's name, the location, the manner of death—it all matched the night that haunted Robert's every waking moment. He could vividly recall the driveway where it had happened, the cold steel of the weapon in his hand, and the final, desperate gasp of the victim.

The judge's voice droned on, recounting the gruesome details of the crime scene. The defendant had been linked to the scene through circumstantial evidence, but Robert knew the truth. He knew that the man sitting in front of him, hunched and defeated, was not the killer.

The realization that his secret, the murder he had committed, was now the centerpiece of this trial, sent a chill down Robert's spine. The trial threatened to unravel everything he had tried to keep hidden.

The judge pronounced other details, such as the names of the lawyers, but Robert had already tuned the judge completely out. He gripped the edge of the jury box, his knuckles whitening. This couldn't be real, he thought. It wasn't possible! The

Earth seemed to have come off its axis as the realization sank in for Robert. This wasn't just any trial – it was his trial, his crime, and an innocent man was now on the verge of potentially paying for Robert's sins. A wave of nausea swept over him as he fought to maintain his composure, the walls of the courtroom closing in like a vice. This was not anything Robert had ever anticipated. How could it be?

Robert had always prided himself on his integrity, his unflinching adherence to the rule of law. But now, as the judge spoke, he felt the weight of his double life pressing down on him. It was suffocating. He needed to run out of the courtroom and breathe in the fresh air of the outside. He tried to regain some composure and listen to the judge again.

"Ladies and gentlemen, before we proceed with the selection process, it is important to determine if there are any reasons why any of you should not serve on this jury …"

Robert's mind raced. Any reason?! Yes, he could think of one. He knew the victim – intimately, considering the circumstances. Was that reason enough?

The image of the man he had killed flashed vividly before his eyes, each detail etched into his memory with brutal clarity. It had been a stormy night, the kind that made the streets slick and treacherous. Robert had been tailing his victim, with the intent to confront him. As he waited in the shadows near the victim's home, he noticed another man leaving the house around midnight. Robert didn't know who the man was or why he was there, but he had to wait for him to leave before making his move. While he waited, he caught sight of a neighbor peering through their window, casting an uneasy glance into the rain-soaked street. As if the rain wasn't enough, two street lights were out and the one dim, flickering streetlight didn't provide enough light for Robert to see clearly, which somewhat alleviated his fears since there would be little that the neighbor could make out with such poor visibility. He watched as the neighbor eventually moved away from the window and the man he had been tailing stepped outside, bringing out the trash and giving him the opportunity he needed.

The confrontation in the driveway escalated quickly, a flurry of shouts and accusations. Robert remembered the struggle, the way the man's eyes widened in panic as he realized the gravity of the situation. The rain-soaked ground had made it more difficult than normal to keep their footing, and they had both struggled somewhat to stay upright, grappling with each other in the wet darkness.

Then, in a heartbeat, it was over. The man had fallen to the ground, his body hitting the driveway with a sickening thud. Robert, his mind racing and his pulse pounding in his ears, had drawn his gun, a Smith & Wesson Model 10. The look of shock on the man's face as he lay there, defenseless, was something Robert would never forget. And then, with a deafening roar, Robert had pulled the trigger twice. The man's body jerked violently. The shots rang out, but it seemed like they blended in with the storm. Robert wasn't sure. Robert watched the life draining from the man's eyes as a pool of blood spread beneath him. The lifelessness that followed was eerie, a stark contrast to the chaos that had preceded it.

This memory, burned into Robert's consciousness, haunted him day and night. He had tried to bury it, to lock it away in the deepest recesses of his mind, but it always found a way to eventually resurface, especially now, with the summons in his hand and in the courthouse.

It wasn't as if he hadn't thought about this over the last two years. But it had become like a dream; it wasn't real anymore. Or so he had convinced himself. But even so, the memory was seared into the back of his brain, always a relentless reminder of his darkest secret. He couldn't sit in judgment when the crime in question was his own?

"Do any of you know the parties involved in this case, either personally or professionally? This includes the defendant, the plaintiff, the attorneys, or any witnesses who may be called to testify. If you recognize any names or faces, please raise your hand."

Robert's heart pounded as he felt his hand twitch at his side. For a moment he thought his hand would have more courage than his heart and it would raise itself. It was a relief to think it might do so. He wanted to stand up and scream that he was the one who should be on trial, not the man sitting at the defense table. The guilt gnawed at him, whispering to him and taunting him that he had no right to judge anyone. But confessing meant throwing away a life of dedication to the law, or certainly the image of it. The thought of prison bars closing in around him was unbearable.

"Do any of you have any personal knowledge about the facts of this case? Have you read or heard anything about this case in the news, or from any other source, that might influence your ability to be impartial?"

The truth bubbled up inside him, desperate for release. How could he sit in judgment of another man when he himself was a murderer? And then he remembered, he was thee murderer! He felt the bile rise in his throat, the room spinning slightly as his heart pounded in his chest. But then he thought of the potential fallout. His reputation would be in shadders.

"Do you have any personal, financial, or professional interest in the outcome of this case?"

He couldn't bear the risks of raising his hand. He couldn't face the consequences, no matter what they were. He looked at the defendant. He knew his type. He wasn't guilty of this crime, Robert was well aware of that, but he was guilty of others. Dressed to the nines. What a joke, he thought. It doesn't quite fit right, does it? Robert had been on the beat too long to be fooled by some fancy getup. He knew that underneath that suit … Then he stopped himself in horror. This was an innocent man, and he knew it. What was he thinking?

Relax, Robert thought. He began to convince himself that maybe he wouldn't even be selected for the jury. But if he was chosen, then he could see who this man really was. If the defendant didn't belong in jail, there was no one better suited to ensure justice than him, sitting on the jury. Yes, that was it! This wasn't a coincidence.

"Are there any other reasons, such as past experiences, personal beliefs, or any other factors, that might affect your ability to be fair and impartial in this case?"

The hand that once wanted to raise on its own had settled comfortably by Robert's side. But still, this decision was settling heavily upon him. As the judge continued, Robert sat still, his face a mask of calm, but inside, he felt like he was falling apart. The irony of his situation was almost too much to bear. He had become the very thing he had once hunted. A criminal hiding in plain sight, about to pass judgment on another. The courtroom moved on, oblivious to his inner turmoil, as Robert silently vowed to see this through, for better or worse. No one raised their hand, including Robert.

Now it was time for the attorneys to ask their questions. Robert sat uncomfortably on the hard wooden chair, not knowing what was to come and feeling the weight of the courtroom's eyes upon him. His hands rested calmly on his lap, but his mind was a storm of thoughts.

The prosecutor, a sharp-eyed woman named Ms. Jennings, stood and approached. She exuded confidence in a tailored navy blazer paired with a sleek pencil skirt, both impeccably fitted. Her crisp, white blouse added a touch of sophistication, complemented by classic black pumps. Every detail, from her minimalist jewelry to her polished briefcase on the table, spoke of professionalism and sharpness. As she moved closer, the subtle scent of her perfume filled the air—feminine yet strong, a blend of floral notes with a hint of spice, perfectly mirroring her poised and assertive demeanor.

"Mr. Carter," she began, her voice clear and authoritative, "I see here in the questionnaire that you filled out that you are a retired police captain. Is that correct?"

Robert nodded. "Yes, ma'am. I served for 25 years."

"Thank you for your service," she said with a polite smile. "Given your background in law enforcement, do you believe you can remain impartial and objective in this case?"

Robert took a measured breath. "Absolutely. My job was always to follow the evidence and uphold the law. I can separate my past profession from my duty as a juror."

Ms. Jennings nodded, appearing satisfied. "Can you assure the court that you will not allow your experiences as a police captain to influence your judgment unfairly?"

"Yes, ma'am," Robert replied, meeting her gaze steadily. "I understand the importance of fairness and justice. I can be impartial." Just then Robert felt like he had choked on his words. But if he had, it seemed like no one else had noticed.

The prosecutor asked a few more simple questions, but it was clear she was convinced. She thanked him and returned to her seat.

Next, the defense attorney, a younger man with an earnest expression, named Mr. Lewis, took his turn. He walked over with a friendly smile. He seemed awkward in his suit, tugging at the lapels like he was embarrassed everyone knew his suit had just been pulled from a clearance bin. The fabric, a coarse blend that did nothing to disguise its synthetic origins, hung poorly on his frame, bagging at the elbows and puckering around the shoulders. The color – a ghastly shade of faded charcoal – seemed to absorb the bad lighting of the courtroom, highlighting every wrinkle and crease. The trousers were slightly too long and slightly too big, but not big enough to hide scuffed, worn-out shoes that managed to peek through. In spite of it all, though, Mr. Lewis stood there with a naive pride.

"Mr. Carter," he began, "you mentioned that you served for 25 years. That must have given you quite a perspective on the criminal justice system."

"It did," Robert acknowledged.

"Do you believe that sometimes the system can make mistakes?"

Robert hesitated for a fraction of a second, a flicker of something unreadable crossing his face. "Yes, I do. No system is perfect. That's why it's important for every juror to weigh the evidence carefully and make sure justice is served."

Mr. Lewis nodded, pleased with the response. "Do you think you can give my client the same presumption of innocence that you would want for yourself or a loved one?"

Robert's mind flashed briefly to the dark secret he carried. He pushed it aside, keeping his expression neutral. "Of course. Everyone deserves that presumption until proven otherwise, beyond all reasonable doubt."

Mr. Lewis smiled. "Thank you, Mr. Carter."

As the defense attorney sat down, Robert felt a strange mix of relief and dread. The attorneys went through the same routine with the others and then the judge asked these members of the jury panel to depart the courtroom, and Robert was left alone with his thoughts.

Part of him felt a twisted sense of security at the potential of being on the jury. He could keep an eye on the proceedings and discover if anything pointed back to him. But another part of him, the part he couldn't quite silence, felt the growing tension of his duplicity. He couldn't tell if it was guilt or fear that troubled him more. As he sat in the lobby of the courthouse, the repetitive buzz of the overhead fluorescent lights droned incessantly, each flicker and hum grating against his already frayed nerves, adding to his growing sense of unease.

As he struggled with his conflicts, a clerk for the judge approached him. She was a tall woman with a stern demeanor, her auburn hair pulled back into a tight bun that seemed to add an extra inch to her already imposing height. Her sharp features were accentuated by the thin, wire-framed glasses perched on her nose, which gave her a no-nonsense look. Dressed in a crisp, white blouse and a navy skirt, she moved with the brisk efficiency of someone who had seen it all and was determined not to be delayed by anything. The stack of papers she held in her arms rustled slightly as she walked, a testament to her endless duties in the courthouse.

Robert's eyes followed her as she made her way through the lobby, her sensible heels clicking on the marble floor. As she got closer, he noticed the way her eyes scanned the room, pinpointing individuals with the precision of a hawk. She glanced down at her clipboard, then back up at him, her expression unchanging.

Robert realized with a jolt that she was probably approaching him to inform him of whether he had been selected as a juror from the jury pool. His stomach churned at the thought, the gravity of the situation weighing on him even more heavily.

The clerk stopped in front of him and extended a form and a crisp, white envelope. "You've been selected for the jury, Mr. Carter. You're lucky juror number 12, the last to be selected. All 12 jurors and one alternate have now been chosen. The trial will start next week Tuesday at 10:30 AM. Orientation will start at 9:00 AM before that but we ask that you arrive a half hour early."

Robert took the form and envelope, his mind racing. The weight of his secret pressed down on him even more, and he forced a nod, trying to maintain a semblance of composure.

As Robert took the form and envelope from the clerk, she directed him with a curt nod towards an office down the hallway.

"Please proceed to the office at the end of the hall," she instructed, her voice firm. "You'll receive further instructions there."

Robert nodded again, clutching the papers tightly, and headed towards the indicated office. His steps felt heavy, each one bringing him closer to a responsibility he wasn't sure he could bear. The hallway stretched out before him, lined with old, framed photographs of the courthouse's history and the judges who had presided over it, the echoes of his footsteps bouncing off the polished floors.

CHAPTER 3

The Trial

Robert sat through the trial in a state of heightened tension, every word, every piece of evidence a reminder of the crime he had committed. From the moment the trial began, he felt like he was watching a macabre play where he knew every line and every scene, but from an angle that twisted his guts.

The prosecutor laid out the case with clinical precision. In her opening statement, she recounted the evening two years ago, describing the victim – a local businessman with no known enemies – found dead in his driveway. The crime scene photos flashed on the screen, each one a dagger to Robert's conscience. He remembered what had driven him to that house, and the irrevocable act that followed. The prosecution had a simple but effective theory: the defendant was in debt to the victim, a botched robbery, a struggle, and ultimately, murder.

In his opening argument, the defense attorney tried highlighting that there was a lack of physical evidence directly linking Daniel to the murder scene. No murder weapon, no DNA.

"Ladies and gentlemen of the jury," he began, pacing before them, "the prosecution has given you a story. But it's just a story. A story filled with holes. Where is the weapon? Where is the DNA? How can we convict without concrete evidence?"

One by one witnesses took the stand, each adding another layer to the narrative. The neighbor who had seen the defendant, Daniel, arguing with the victim that night was the first to testify.

"I saw them from my window," the neighbor said, her voice trembling slightly. "It was around midnight. They were shouting at each other. It looked heated."

"What did you hear, exactly?" the prosecutor asked, her tone steady and controlled.

The neighbor hesitated, glancing at Daniel before continuing. "I couldn't make out the words and then I went back to bed before they had stopped their arguing."

Next was a passerby who claimed to have heard shouts but couldn't identify the voices. His testimony was less compelling, yet the prosecutor used specific questions to bolster the timeline.

"I was walking my dog around midnight," the passerby answered to a question from the prosecutor. "My dog's terrified of lightning and thunder, so if I don't go out walking with him he won't go out and do his business on his own. As we were walking, I heard some yelling from the driveway, but I couldn't see anyone – my view was obstructed. But I heard two men arguing."

The prosecutor introduced a series of text messages between the victim and an unknown number, for which the prosecution had already provided evidence that inconclusively linked Daniel to the number, discussing a debt.

"These messages," she said, pointing to the screen where the texts were displayed, "show a clear motive. The victim was pressuring Daniel to repay a significant sum of money. That's why he robbed him and killed him – out of anger."

Robert couldn't believe how neatly the pieces fit together, as if fate itself were conspiring against Daniel. He felt the weight of his own actions more acutely with each passing moment.

Daniel's defense attorney fought valiantly, if hopelessly, trying to cast doubt wherever possible. He asked questions that pointed out the inconsistencies in the prosecution's timeline, suggesting that the real killer was, in fact, still out there.

Despite his best efforts, it was clear that his grasp on the complexities of the case was, at best, tenuous. His arguments, while passionate, often lacked the depth and precision needed to counter the prosecution's well-constructed narrative. Robert, sitting in the jury box, couldn't help but notice the attorney's occasional stumbles over key details and his reliance on broad generalities rather than on concrete facts. It was not an indictment of his character, but an observation of his professional limitations. And Robert couldn't help but notice how the defense attorney's arguments seemed to be falling on deaf ears in the jury.

The defense attorney did his best to undermine the credibility of the prosecution's key witnesses.

"You said you heard shouting," he questioned one witness. "But can you be certain it was Daniel you saw? It was dark, wasn't it?"

The neighbor wavered, but her initial certainty seemed to diminish slightly. "I think it was him. Yes, I'm pretty sure."

Robert thought to himself, the defense attorney will press hard on this witness now. He can undermine their entire testimony. Instead, his performance was utterly lackluster.

"Pretty sure isn't enough for a conviction," the defense attorney pressed, though the impact of his questioning seemed minimal.

The trial featured a parade of prosecution witnesses, each adding layers to the prosecution's meticulously constructed narrative. There was the prosecution's forensic expert, for one, who detailed the fibers found on the victim, linking them to a type of jacket owned by the defendant. Then there were eyewitnesses who testified that they saw heated arguments and suspicious activity on the night of the murder.

Throughout the proceedings, the prosecutor delivered blow after blow, presenting evidence with clinical precision and unwavering confidence. On the other hand, the defense attorney struggled, his attempts to introduce doubt falling short.

As the trial continued, the defense brought in forensic experts to discuss the lack of physical evidence. But the prosecutor's line of questions pushed back. "This wasn't a spur-of-the-moment crime," the prosecutor countered. "This was premeditated. The absence of physical evidence does not equate to innocence." She pushed this narrative effectively with the questioning of each witness.

Throughout the trial, Robert's mind was a storm of conflicting emotions. He watched as the scales of justice tipped precariously, aware that his own actions had set this entire sequence in motion. He knew that his confession could change everything.

As the trial neared its end, the defense attorney made a final, desperate plea to the jury. "I ask you to consider the lack of concrete evidence. I ask you to consider the possibility that Daniel is innocent. The prosecution's narrative is just that – a narrative. It's your duty to see through it." His efforts, however, struggled to weave a compelling story of his client's innocence. What few points he made effectively seemed to be lost on the jury. "Consider the timeline," he said, his voice rising with conviction. "The eyewitnesses have differing accounts as to when the murder took place that night."

In stark contrast, the prosecutor's closing statement was delivered with confidence and assurance. "We have shown motive, opportunity, and behavior consistent with guilt. Daniel has no alibi for the time of the murder and was placed at the scene by witnesses. He must be held accountable for his actions." The jurors around Robert were captivated by the prosecutor's narrative. It seemed as though deliberations were not going to take long.

As the trial concluded, Robert's mind raced.

He replayed every moment of that fateful night, every choice that had led him to this courtroom. The weight of his guilt was overwhelming, but he knew that stepping forward now was not an option. Yet not stepping forward felt like a knife to his very soul. It had to resolve this conflict.

The judge gave final instructions to the jury, his voice steady and authoritative. Near the end, he emphasized, "Remember, your duty is to weigh the evidence impartially and deliver a verdict based solely on what has been presented in this courtroom. Justice must be blind, and your decisions must be grounded in truth."

These words struck a chord deep within Robert, resonating with an almost painful clarity. As the trial ended, Robert filed out with the other jurors, fulling understanding the enormity of what lay ahead: whether to let an innocent man pay for his crime, as it seemed likely that the jury was convinced of the defendant's guilt, or, if necessary, to confess to save this innocent man and then face the ruin of his own life.

The judge's final words echoed in his mind, "deliver a verdict based solely on what has been presented in this courtroom." This directive haunted Robert, highlighting the stark contradiction between his hidden past and the responsibility now placed upon him. He knew the truth, which had not been presented in this courtroom. He realized that the concept of truth was not just a legal formality but a moral imperative, one that he could no longer ignore without devastating consequences. But he was still confused as to what direction he should take.

The jury was then sent to deliberate. As the jury filed into the deliberation room, Robert felt a knot tighten in his stomach. He had hoped that, once behind closed doors, some semblance of doubt might emerge among his fellow jurors, despite the uninspired performance of the defense attorney. But he was also conflicted. Maybe it would be better if the defendant was found guilty.

CHAPTER 4

Guilty

One by one, the jurors entered the deliberation room and settled into their seats. They were eyeing each other with a mix of curiosity and apprehension. The room was cold and utilitarian. Not literally cold but rather without any character. There was a long rectangular table in the center of the room. Around it sat twelve padded chairs that looked to Robert as though they had been there for decades. Fluorescent lights cast a harsh glow over the room, emphasizing the wear and tear on the institutional green walls. A whiteboard hung at one end, its surface marred with the markings of past deliberations. A clock on the opposite wall seemed to tick loudly, marking the passing of each tense second. You could literally smell the history of the room. There was a heady mix of oak and leather, mingling with a faint, musty scent that hinted at years of intense, hushed conversations.

Among the jurors sat a diverse array of individuals, a microcosm of the community they represented. Young and old, male and female, a tapestry of races and ethnicities woven together in this room of judgment. Each juror brought their own unique perspective, setting the stage for a complex and nuanced deliberation. Their differences, once seemingly insignificant, would soon become magnified in the charged atmosphere of deliberation, each juror a unique voice in the search for justice. They would soon learn that nothing was insignificant in their deliberations.

The judge had provided instructions that, unless the juror declined, Juror 1 would serve as the jury foreperson by default. Juror 1, a nervous young man named Blake, quickly made it clear he did not want this responsibility. Without hesitation, the jury began discussing the process of selecting a new foreperson. After a brief exchange, Juror 8, a middle-aged man with a calm demeanor and an authoritative presence, emerged as the consensus choice. His confidence and steady gaze reassured the others, and they hoped his leadership would guide them through the difficult deliberations ahead.

The new foreperson had a certain gravitas about him. His blond hair and neatly trimmed beard gave him an air of wisdom, and his piercing blue eyes seemed to look right through you, assessing but understanding. He wore a crisp, white shirt and a navy blazer, exuding an aura of professionalism and integrity. There was something in the way he carried himself — an unspoken confidence that came from years of experience, perhaps as an executive, someone used to making decisions and leading others. As he took his place at the head of the table, the other jurors felt a collective sense of relief, as if they had found a captain to steer them through the stormy seas ahead.

With the foreperson appointed, Juror 8 wasted no time in guiding the group. He addressed the jury, informing them that their deliberations were scheduled for weekdays between 9:00 AM and 4:30 PM. Within those hours, he, as the foreperson, had the authority to call breaks and could also recess the deliberations for the day earlier than 4:30, provided he informed the judge. However, if the jury wished to extend their deliberations beyond 4:30, he would need to send a note to the judge with such a request. Most of this was already explained to the members of the jury during their orientation.

After informing everyone of this, the foreperson quickly directed the jurors as to what he considered the first order of business: a quick vote to see where they stood as a group – a 'gut feel' vote, as he called it. Caroline, Juror 3, politely suggested a secret ballot because she thought it was important that each juror could express their opinion without fear of judgment or influence. The jurors nodded in agreement.

Amara, Juror 7, disagreed gently but firmly. "I get where you're comin' from, Caroline, but I think we gotta stand behind what we believe in. With somethin' this important, we need transparency."

Caroline nodded, acknowledging Amara's point. "I see your point, hun, but my concern is that some jurors might feel pressured to go along with the majority if we vote openly. A secret ballot allows for honesty without fear of judgment."

Amara responded, her tone respectful but firm, perhaps more firm than before. "I hear you, but I think it's crucial we know where everyone stands right from the start. We need to be open and transparent."

The foreperson intervened, sensing the growing debate. "You both make valid points, but we need to move forward. I'll call for yeas and nays on whether we'll have a secret ballot and we'll let the majority rule on this. All in favor of a secret ballot, say 'yea.'"

A chorus of "yeas" filled the room, with a few "nays" following that when the foreperson called for them.

"The yeas have it," the foreperson declared. "We'll conduct a secret ballot." Slips of paper were then distributed for the jurors to write down their verdicts.

Once all the votes were cast, the foreperson collected and organized them in silence. With a solemn voice, he began to read out the results, starting with the first ballot. "Guilty," he said, then moved on to the second. "Guilty," he repeated, and continued down the line until all the ballots had been read — each one the same: guilty.

Robert's heart sank as the weight of their decision settled on him — his decision. What had he done? Was that it? An innocent man was going to be found guilty? Panic surged within him. He should have voted not guilty, he thought. He hadn't realized it all could end so quickly.

Shock coursed through him like a live wire had

fallen on him, his mind reeling with disbelief. How could they all be so sure of Daniel's guilt when the flaws of every piece of evidence gnawed at Robert like a pack of hungry wolves? There was reasonable doubt everywhere.

As the weight of their decision settled over the room, Robert felt a sickening sense of despair wash over him. He was torn between the need to protect himself and the desire to see justice served. In that moment, he faced a choice that would define him: to stand alone in defense of an innocent man or to succumb to the darkness of his own guilt and let the defendant be found guilty.

Robert spoke, trying to steer the deliberation in a more meticulous direction. "Let's go over all of the evidence. We owe the defendant that. Then let's vote again after that."

Amara frowned, her voice carrying the cadence of her African-American heritage. "Why we gotta drag this out, Robert? We all know what we saw and heard at trial. Ain't no point in rehashing every little detail."

Robert, maintaining his composure, replied, "I understand where you're coming from, Amara. But this is a man's life we're talking about. We need to be thorough."

Amara crossed her arms, her tone firm but respectful. "We've been here for days already with this trial, Robert. You think we missed something? If you ax me, we've seen all there is to see."

Robert shook his head. "I don't think it's about missing something. It's about making sure we all understand the evidence the same way. A man's freedom is at stake, and we owe it to him to be certain."

Amara sighed, glancing around the room. "And what makes you so sure goin' over it again is gonna change anything? We all got eyes and ears. We all know what we saw and heard during the trial."

Before the exchange could escalate further, the foreperson interjected. "Alright, let's hold on a minute," he said, raising a hand to call for attention. "We're here to ensure that justice is served. Our job is to carefully consider all the evidence presented to us before reaching a verdict. We need to be as objective and thorough as possible. This is a serious responsibility."

He looked around the room, meeting the eyes of each juror. "Let's go over all the evidence, piece by piece. We owe it to the defendant, to the court, and to ourselves to make sure we reach a fair and just decision. After that, we can take another vote. Agreed?"

There were murmurs of agreement around the table, and Robert could see a few nods of assent. Even Amara gave a reluctant nod, though her expression remained skeptical.

Robert felt a wave of relief. The extra time would allow him to gather his thoughts and decide his next steps. As the jurors began to review the evidence, he knew he had bought himself some much-needed time to consider what he needed to do.

What lay before him was a monumental task: persuading eleven people that a man they were convinced was guilty actually was not. He knew that, in all likelihood, this task would prove too difficult. And if he couldn't accomplish it, he'd have no choice but to confess. He couldn't let an innocent man go to jail for his crime. But he'd cross that bridge when he came to it. For now, he had one task: convince eleven jurors that the defendant was innocent.

The jurors settled in, pulling out their notes and arranging the evidence on the table. The foreperson organized the discussion, starting with the forensic evidence. They meticulously examined the fibers found on the victim, debating whether they definitively linked the defendant to the crime.

Amara, though skeptical, participated actively. "I just don't see how anyone else coulda done it," she said, shaking her head. "All the signs point to him."

Robert took a deep breath. "We need to be thorough. If there's even a small doubt, we have to explore it."

Convincing eleven people to set aside their beliefs and consider a different perspective was no small feat. He was still unsure that was the correct course of action. But what else could he do? The enormity of the task weighed heavily on him. Perhaps he couldn't accomplish it even if he tried, even if he wanted to. For now, though, he had managed to buy some time.

CHAPTER 5

Committed

The foreperson nodded his head in agreement. "OK, let's review everything we have. It's our duty to deliberate thoroughly and ensure that we haven't overlooked any important details. We need to go over each piece of evidence carefully, discuss it, and understand it fully. Only then can we reach a fair and just verdict. Let's make sure we consider all angles and perspectives before making our final decision of guilt or innocence."

Amara leaned forward, fingers tapping rhythmically on the oak table as she spoke, clearly not entirely happy at the direction they were proceeding in. "Alright, let's break down the witness testimony from the neighbor who spotted the defendant near the victim's home on the night of the murder. The neighbor said he saw the defendant dipping out around midnight, looking shook. That's pretty damning if you ax me. It places him at the scene right when the crime went down. How can we ignore that?"

The room fell silent as the jurors mulled over Amara's point. Then a couple of jurors mumbled, "It's true." Robert could feel the weight of the accusation settling heavily in the room. Before he could decide what he should do he found himself speaking about the flaw in this seemingly solid piece of evidence. It was like it was instinctive for him to speak the truth. In his years of experience in law enforcement, he would often surgically dismantle flawed evidence with his razor-sharp logic, finely tuned over the years.

"Let's pause for a moment," Robert interjected, his voice measured but inquisitive. "Think about what the neighbor said. He mentioned it was midnight, right? Now, why would he be peering out his window at that hour? Seems a bit odd, doesn't it? And he talked about how dark it was. But let's be real, how much can you really see in the dead of night, especially from a distance?"

"Yet," Robert continued, his brow furrowing in thought. "There's more to consider. The neighbor's account leaves out some key details. Can we really trust his memory, especially in the dead of night? And what about misinterpretation? Maybe what he thought he saw was just a trick of the light or something innocent. We've got to take his story with a grain of salt."

Amara mumbled something while crossing

her arms. "The neighbor had a clear view. Said he saw the defendant at the scene, and he swears down it was him."

Robert glanced across the table at Amara, taking in her presence, maybe for the first time. She was a middle-aged Black woman with an air of resilience about her. Her eyes, sharp and intelligent, hinted at a lifetime of challenges overcome. Her hands, strong and calloused, rested confidently on the table, betraying years of hard work. Dressed neatly in professional attire, she carried herself with a dignified poise. Robert couldn't help but respect the strength she emanated, knowing that his experience on the force had shown him firsthand the kind of hardships she had likely faced and surmounted.

"Maybe so," Robert conceded, "but did he describe the lighting conditions? Streetlights? Porch lights? No one asked him anything about that. Was there enough light to see the defendant's face clearly at midnight, or was he relying on the figure and general appearance? Remember, it's not uncommon for people to misidentify someone in poor lighting conditions."

Caroline, with glasses perched on her nose, interjected. "But bless your heart, sugah, that neighbor knew the defendant like the back of his hand. They done lived in the same neighborhood for years. Surely he could recognize him. Shoot, I'd recognize every darn one of my neighbors from a mile away!"

Robert nodded in agreement. "True, but as I mentioned earlier, we lack details on the lighting conditions. It could have been pitch dark for all we know. In such circumstances, even distinguishing a friend from a foe becomes challenging. Trust me, after 25 years in law enforcement, I've encountered numerous instances where eyewitness testimony proved unreliable, especially in low-light conditions. I've learned not to place undue reliance on it, but rather to use it as a starting point for more concrete evidence. Additionally, consider the time frame – how certain was the neighbor about it being precisely midnight? Could it have been earlier or later? The prosecution's timeline has a lot of issues. No one questioned this witness on their certainty about the time. We cannot convict someone based on dubious identification."

Amara's eyes narrowed as she leaned in, her voice edged with frustration. "Listen, Robert, it seems like you're trying to spin things to sow doubt where there ain't none. I see your game. The neighbor testified they saw the defendant. That's the evidence – hard evidence. It ain't 'bout the lighting; it's 'bout the fact that someone who knew the defendant saw him there when the murder went down. Are you saying we should just brush that off?"

The foreman rose from his chair and began to pace, his expression contemplative. "That's not what Robert is saying at all. What you're saying, and tell me if I'm wrong, is that we can't be entirely sure the neighbor's testimony is accurate enough to place the defendant at the scene beyond a reasonable doubt. They could be mistaken."

"Exactly," Robert replied. "We need to scrutinize every piece of evidence with the same critical eye. If there's a reasonable chance the neighbor was mistaken, even if it is small, we can't use that testimony as the foundation for a guilty verdict. We owe it to ourselves and the defendant to be absolutely sure."

The room fell silent, the weight of Robert's words sinking in. Jurors exchanged glances, some nodding slightly in agreement. The foreperson stopped pacing and looked at his watch, then at the tired faces around the table. He sighed to himself as he was preparing to speak.

"Alright, everyone," he said, his voice steady but firm. "It's been a long day, and I think we've made some significant progress. But we're all tired, and we're not going to make any good decisions when we're exhausted. I'm going to recess the deliberations until Monday morning. This will give us all a chance to rest and come back with fresh minds."

A murmur of relief spread through the room. Some jurors stretched, others began to gather their belongings. The foreperson continued, "We'll meet back here at 9:00 AM sharp on Monday. I want everyone to take this time to think about what we've discussed. Remember, we're dealing with someone's life here, and we need to get it right."

Robert felt a mixture of relief and anxiety.

The break would give him time to clear his head, but the weight of the decision still loomed over him. As the jurors filed out of the room, he lingered behind, deep in thought.

"Robert," the foreperson said, approaching him. "You've raised some important points today. Let's keep that momentum going on Monday."

Robert nodded, appreciating the foreperson's acknowledgment. "Thanks. I just want to make sure we're doing the right thing."

"We all do," the foreperson replied. "See you Monday."

Robert gathered his things and headed for the door, the echo of the day's deliberations following him into the weekend as he headed for the exit.

❖ ❖ ❖

For Robert, a profound realization dawned on him as he drove home from the courthouse. He had turned the radio off, so now the rhythmic thrum of the engine was the backdrop to the whirlwind of thoughts swirling in his mind. It was as if he finally was facing what he always knew he needed to do. He could no longer ignore the gnawing sense of responsibility deep within him. The weight of his own guilt had shifted, morphing into a fierce determination to prevent an innocent man from suffering the consequences of his actions.

He glanced at the rearview mirror, half-expecting to see the ghost of the man he had killed sitting in the back seat, silently judging him. The memory of that night was as vivid as if it had happened yesterday. The panic, the rage, the confusion that had driven him to that house. He laughed bitterly, shaking his head at the irony of it all: a murderer who was just and honest. But if people knew what motivated him to kill, they'd understand that apparent contradiction. He wasn't a cold-blooded killer.

As he turned onto his street, the familiar sight of his house brought a sense of relief, even if it would only be temporary. He pulled into the driveway and sat there for a moment, the engine idling. He just needed a few more minutes to keep stretching things out. He thought about the jurors, about how he had planted the seeds of doubt in their minds. He realized what he probably knew all along: he wanted the defendant to be found not guilty. He was committed to this course of action, driven by a need to atone for his own sins in the only way he knew how. There was no other choice for him.

Finally, he killed the engine and stepped out of his car. He took in a breath of the cool night air, trying to clear his mind. He walked up to his front door, the familiar creak of the hinges greeting him as he stepped inside.

Robert headed to the kitchen as his dog desperately tried to get his attention, and poured himself a glass of water. His thoughts were still racing in his head. He sat at the table, staring at the glass in his one hand while petting his dog with his other hand. The deliberation was far from over. He knew that. But a crucial point had been made: the jurors needed to meticulously examine every piece of evidence. He had to keep pushing, keep questioning, until there was no doubt left in anyone's mind. Of course he knew the defendant was innocent. But he needed to convince everyone else of that.

He got up and walked to the living room, sinking into his favorite armchair. The stress of the day had tired him out, but he knew he couldn't rest just yet. The memory of his own crime loomed large in his mind, a constant reminder of his own failings. But now, he had a chance to make things right, at least in some small way. He had to prevent an innocent man from suffering the consequences of his actions. This was the key to bringing things back to normal for him.

He closed his eyes, trying to summon the strength he needed for Monday and the days that would surely follow. He could see the faces of the jurors, hear their voices as they debated and discussed the evidence. He had to keep fighting, keep pushing. It was the only way he could atone for his sins, it was the only way to find some semblance of peace.

As he sat there, he made a silent vow. He would do everything in his power to ensure that justice was served. He would make sure every piece of evidence was examined, question every assumption, until there was no doubt left about the defendant's innocence. He owed it to the defendant, to the other jurors, and to himself.

Robert took another deep breath and stood up. He had a long road ahead of him, but he was ready for the challenge. He walked to the window and looked out into the neighborhood. He felt a renewed sense of purpose, a determination to see this through to the end.

He needed to take the weekend to relax and then on Monday he would be ready to face things head-on again. He would go back to that jury room re-energized and then continue the fight for justice, driven by a need to make things right. The weight of his own guilt was still there, but now it was tempered by a fierce resolve to do what was right. He would not let an innocent man pay for his sins. He would see this through, no matter what it took.

CHAPTER 6

A Shift

Monday morning came quickly. The jurors filtered into the deliberation room, the weight of Friday's discussions still lingering in the air as if it had stayed there even as they had left for the weekend. Each juror carried with them the heavy burden of the case, evident in their somber expressions and slow movements. The room, filled with the muted sounds of chairs scraping and papers rustling, seemed to hold a palpable tension. The morning sunlight streamed through the windows, casting long shadows on the table. As they settled into their seats, the atmosphere was thick with newfound resolve to examine the case and the anticipation of the challenging discussions that lay ahead as a result. They entered the room this Monday morning much more aware of the seriousness of their task then when deliberations had begun. As a result, it was almost as though the room felt smaller, more confined. The weekend had offered little respite; the case had remained at the forefront of their minds. Now, gathered once more, they would soon dive back into the arduous process of seeking truth and justice.

Robert made his way to the coffee pot, nodding to Caroline as she joined him. He poured himself a cup, the rich aroma offering him a small comfort. The scent was a welcoming blend of roasted beans, with earthy undertones and a subtle hint of chocolate, filling the room with a sense of warmth. He took a sip, the warmth spreading through his body, re-energizing him. The coffee was strong, with a slightly bitter taste that had a hint of caramel. It was better than he had expected, grounding him amidst the tension in the room and helping him brace for the day's discussions.

Caroline turned to Robert, her expression thoughtful. "You know, Robert, I have to admit that I was quite surprised to receive the summons for jury duty."

Robert chuckled wryly. "I was surprised too, Caroline. You have no idea how surprised I really was."

She smiled, a hint of nostalgia in her eyes. "I had only just returned from livin' in Europe for three years. The very first day I checked my mail, there it was – a letter for jury duty. My goodness!"

Robert raised an eyebrow, intrigued. "Three

years in Europe? What were you doing over there?"

Caroline sighed softly and began to lean against the wall. "I went to Italy, presumably to find myself."

Robert nodded, encouraging her to continue.

"Robert," she began, her voice earnest, "I've lived a privileged life. I know that. But I've had hardships as well. After my time in Italy I eventually admitted that most, if not all, of my hardships were of my own makin'. The first year in Italy, it was difficult to adapt. After that, you adjust and start takin' on their way of livin', in some ways even their way of thinkin'. It was three years of blissful eatin' and drinkin'. Robert, I love Italy."

Robert smiled, genuinely curious. "Did you find what you were looking for?" Caroline's face clouded with a momentary confusion. Robert leaned forward. "Did you find yourself?"

She laughed softly, almost self-deprecatingly. "Oh, that! You know, instead of finding myself I think I found a new me. But only after I forgave myself for all the bad decisions I've made in my life. It seems I can forgive others easily, but it's more difficult forgivin' myself. But I can't have those decisions hangin' on my neck like an albatross my whole life. It took three years, but eventually I forgave myself. I finally realized I couldn't move on until I admitted that, for me, most of my hardships were largely the result of my own decisions. It was once I admitted to that, somethin'

I really knew all along but wouldn't face, that I was able to start to move forward. I feel like I still have some work to do. But Robert, I'm a new woman!"

Robert looked at her, admiring the strength she had found. "That's quite a journey, Caroline. I'm glad you found your peace."

She nodded, her eyes shining with a mix of relief and determination. "Thank you, Robert. It means a lot to me to be able to share that with you. It feels good to do that." Then, as if she had almost forgotten about it, she asked Robert, "Did you notice Sheriff Hogan in the courtroom every day last week? He was there from the beginning of the trial to the end."

"Yeah, I saw him," Robert replied, his tone warm and conversational. "Always sitting in the back, attentively watching everything."

As the two of them stood there, making small talk, Robert realized they had more in common than just their presence on the jury. They both hailed from small towns, shared a love for Italian food, and had a penchant for early-morning cups of coffee. They exchanged anecdotes about their hometowns, reminiscing about simpler times and shared experiences. Caroline had a relaxed demeanor and Robert found himself enjoying their conversation more than he had anticipated.

Amidst their discussion, Robert's thoughts drifted back to Sheriff Hogan. The man had a quiet, rugged demeanor, the kind of presence that spoke volumes without uttering a word. His sidearm peeked through his coat as he walked. It didn't seem to match the standard issue sidearms Robert was used to, but there was still something familiar. It was a small detail, easily overlooked, but for some reason, it stood out like a sore thumb to Robert.

The Sheriff seemed like the salt-of-the-earth type – honest, straightforward, maybe even a bit too straightforward for Robert's liking. But smart. The Sheriff's piercing gaze had often settled on Robert, and he couldn't help but wonder what the man was thinking. Did he suspect something? Or was he just another observer?

Caroline fixed her hair as she turned to Robert, her voice filled with warmth and understanding. "Well, let's get back to it, y'all," she said kindly. Robert nodded, and they both walked back to the table, joining the other jurors who were already seated.

The foreperson stood up and cleared his throat, signaling the start of the new day of deliberations. Caroline remarked to everyone, "We're here to do our duty, but remember, we're all feeling the weight of this responsibility. If anyone needs a moment or has something to share, we're here for each other." Her words were a gentle reminder of their shared humanity and the importance of supporting one another through the deliberation process.

"Thank you, Caroline. Good morning, everyone," the foreperson began, his tone firm yet encouraging. "Let's pick up where we left off yesterday. There's still a lot to discuss, and we need to make sure we cover every piece of evidence thoroughly. Remember, our responsibility here is to seek the truth, regardless of any preconceived notions or personal biases. Let's keep an open mind, respect each other's viewpoints, and work together to ensure a fair and just outcome. Now, let's get started."

The discussion meandered for a while, with no real purpose. Sometimes it would seem like they were about to talk about some crucial part of the case. But instead, they probably spent over an hour on the mundane parts of the case. Robert sat stoically in his chair, saying nothing. He felt as though the more upright he sat in his chair the less likely he was to speak. He didn't dare speak because he had this foreboding feeling that if he opened his mouth a confession would just fall out.

Robert was about to scream at the banality of the discussion – screaming isn't speaking, is it? – when Theresa, who had also been completely quiet until now, spoke up. "There's something we haven't really talked about yet that's important. The defendant's fingerprints were found on the victim's car door. That seems pretty solid to me. As the prosecutor said, it places him at the scene of the crime and connects him directly to the victim."

A murmur of agreement rippled through the room. Robert wanted to speak but held himself back, deathly afraid he was going to confess.

Theresa continued, "I mean, how do you

explain that away? It's not like your fingerprints can just appear out of nowhere."

Robert felt a new unease stir within him. He knew that he needed to keep quiet. Let them sort this out. Surely they'll figure out the weakness of the evidence on their own. But he couldn't let this piece of evidence go unchallenged. No one was speaking against it.

Robert took the time to gain his composure, then he leaned forward. He could hear a slight crack as he did this, like a sign he had sat upright and still for far too long. He felt like a piece of laundry left on the clothesline overnight, stiffened into an icy relic by the morning frost and cracked out of the shape it had formed into.

"Alright, let's think about this for a moment. The prosecutor cleverly implied this evidence places the defendant at the scene of the crime. But it doesn't. Fingerprints only show that someone touched an object at some point in time. It doesn't tell us when it happened. The defendant and the victim knew each other, right? They lived in the same neighborhood."

Caroline nodded, adding, "They sure did, sugah. Remember, the defendant and victim knew each other casually."

"Exactly," Robert said, seizing the opening. "So, it's entirely possible that the defendant touched the car at some earlier time. Maybe they had a conversation by the car, maybe the defendant leaned on it while talking to the victim. There's no way to pin down the exact moment those fingerprints were left."

Amara, clearly frustrated, interjected, "Maybe, maybe, maybe. There you go again, Robert, flipping the script! Always finding some way to throw shade on everything. It's clear the fingerprints are pointing fingers. My prints ain't on that whip. Your prints ain't on that whip. But the defendant's are! You're just trying to muddy the waters."

Before Robert could respond, Caroline spoke up, her voice calm but firm. "Now, Amara, it don't matter none if you reckon Robert's twisting things. He's raised a valid point and that's what matters. Fingerprints don't come attached with timestamps. We can't rightly say when they were left on the car. It might've been innocent contact from days or weeks before the crime."

The foreperson nodded in agreement. "Caroline is right. We have to be certain beyond a reasonable doubt. I'm not saying he's innocent. But if there's any plausible explanation for the evidence that doesn't involve the defendant committing the crime, we have to consider it."

As Caroline's voice trembled with uncertainty, echoing the doubts that lingered in the minds of many, she reiterated the sentiment of the foreperson. "Exactly. Any explanation that doesn't pin the crime on the defendant, we ought to give it due consideration." Then, with a newfound confidence, she posed a compelling question. "What if the defendant's been set up to take the fall? It's not unheard of for someone to be framed."

Robert shifted uncomfortably in his seat, his heart pounding in his chest. This was not what he wanted. The suggestion of someone framing the defendant sent a shiver down his spine, a haunting reminder of the secrets he harbored. His eyes darted around the room, searching for any sign that his fellow jurors suspected the truth.

Amara, her voice carrying the weight of her convictions, seized the opportunity to sow seeds of doubt on this new theory. "Hold on now," she interjected, her tone sharp and insistent, "before we start conjuring up all sorts of fanciful tales, let's stick to the facts. Ain't nobody got time for wild guesses and fairy tales." Her eyes narrowed as they briefly met Robert's, a silent challenge lingering in the air. "We're here to find justice, not play make-believe." The tension between them crackled in the air, a silent battle of wills that threatened to boil over at any moment.

Robert's internal conflict intensified as he found himself in an uncommon alignment with Amara. While he didn't want the defendant to be found guilty, the notion of the jury considering an alternative culprit, even for a moment, filled him with trepidation. The unexpected convergence of their viewpoints, though surprising, didn't alleviate the underlying tension between the two.

Tom, preparing to speak for the first time, turned to Caroline, curiosity etched across his features. "So, Caroline, what do you suggest we do?"

Caroline's gaze shifted to Robert, who felt the weight of her scrutiny like a physical force. Robert hesitated, torn between his desire to assist the defendant and the instinct to safeguard his own secret. After a pregnant pause, he spoke, his voice measured and deliberate, masking the turmoil raging within him.

"As I've said before, there's only one thing for us to do. Let's go over the evidence in an orderly way and with a fine-tooth comb. Let's look for any inconsistencies, any holes in the prosecution's case. But let's also be cautious about jumping to conclusions about other suspects. We need to be thorough, but we also need to consider the implications of our theories," Robert urged.

Amidst the lively discussion, Robert's gaze wandered around the deliberation room, taking in its bleak surroundings. It was then that he noticed for the first time – really noticed – the table they had been sitting at, standing out amidst the drabness of the room like a beacon of elegance. Crafted from rich oak, its polished surface gleamed under the harsh fluorescent lights, casting a warm, inviting glow.

The table was a striking contrast to the room's institutional furnishings, its intricate carvings and ornate legs hinting at a bygone era of craftsmanship. It must have been an antique, Robert surmised, its timeless beauty standing in stark contrast to the sterile surroundings. And there was still that lingering smell of history in the room, telling silent tales of countless deliberations that had taken place over the years.

As he admired the table's exquisite design, Robert couldn't help but feel a sense of reverence wash over him. It was as if the table held on its sturdy frame the weight of history, a silent witness to the countless deliberations that had taken place around its surface. It seemed as though the most hallowed part of the room was around this table, where countless juries held in their hands the fate of those accused. And that seemed fitting.

Lost in contemplation, Robert returned his focus to the ongoing discussion, the hum of debate filling the room like a symphony of voices. Each juror contributed their own thoughts and opinions to the mix, their words echoing off the walls in a cacophony of ideas and arguments.

One by one, they revisited the testimonies of the eyewitnesses. Some jurors began to waver, questioning their initial certainty as they re-examined each piece of evidence in detail. Robert noticed subtle shifts in their body language and expressions.

Robert listened intently, his mind racing as he struggled to navigate the delicate balance between truth and self-preservation. With each passing moment, the weight of his conscience grew heavier, urging him to confront the truth lurking in the shadows of his past. But as the discussion raged on, Robert found himself torn between the desire for redemption and the fear of what lay ahead.

The foreperson's steady guidance kept the

discussion focused and respectful. "Let's keep our minds open and look at this from every angle," he reminded them. "We have a duty to be fair and impartial."

As the morning wore on, the room filled with the hum of quiet deliberation. The tension gradually gave way to a more collaborative atmosphere. Robert's once unlikely hope for an acquittal grew into a glimmer of hope. Maybe, just maybe, he could sway the jurors to see the possibility of the defendant's innocence. But as the morning drew to a close, Robert knew the real challenge lay ahead.

"Lunch time," announced the foreperson. "We'll start again in one hour."

CHAPTER 7

The Confession?

The jurors dispersed for lunch, each finding their own corner of the room to eat or stepping out to get a breath of fresh air. Robert opted for a simple sandwich and coffee, sitting alone by a window. The sandwich, though basic, had a satisfying blend of fresh, crisp lettuce and savory, well-seasoned turkey, with a hint of mustard that added a pleasant tang. He watched the hustle and bustle of the city outside, his mind momentarily drifting away from the tensions of the deliberation room. Around him, snippets of mundane conversations filled the air – Chester chatting about his favorite teams with Tom, and Betty scrolling through a phone, occasionally sharing amusing pics with the foreperson.

As the lunch break wound down, Robert observed Caroline and Amara engaged in a lively discussion about their favorite local restaurants. Their laughter filled the room as they reminisced about past dining experiences and exchanged opinions on the best dishes in town.

"Y'all ever been to Mama Belle's Diner?" Caroline drawled, her Southern accent thicker than normal. "I swear, the aroma of that crispy fried chicken could pull me in from a mile away. It's just like my nanny used to make. And their biscuits and gravy. Oh-my-Lord!"

Amara nodded, her eyes lighting up. "Oh, I know exactly what you mean, girl. I've been there. But you really have to try Miss Lula's collard greens. They just melt in your mouth. And those ribs? Lord, have mercy, they just fall right off the bone."

Caroline laughed, a melodic sound that made the whole room feel a little lighter. "Oh, don't even get me started. Yes, ma'am, I've been to Miss Lula's! I can't get enough of those collard greens. And the way she seasons those ribs? It's like a little piece of heaven on a plate."

Robert listened in, intrigued by their animated conversation. He had never seen two people speak so passionately about food. Caroline continued, "You know, there's something so comforting about good Southern cooking. It's like every bite takes you back home."

Amara agreed wholeheartedly. "Absolutely. It's not just food, it's an experience. It's 'bout tradition and love. If it ain't cooked with love it won't taste good. That's what makes it special."

Their discussion was a delightful mix of culinary passion and shared memories, providing a brief respite from the weighty deliberations of the trial. Robert couldn't help but feel a bit surprised; he'd never realized how food could bring people together so effortlessly. As their chatter continued, it became evident that it wasn't just the food making them so animated. They were happy to find common ground, forging unexpected connections amidst the tension of the jury room.

The ordinary nature of these moments provided a brief respite from the weighty task ahead. With the clock ticking closer to the end of their break, the jurors began to trickle back into the deliberation room, their casual demeanor gradually giving way to the solemn duty they were about to resume.

The foreperson called the deliberations back to order and Alice, a meticulous older woman who, based on her attire, seemed to have a penchant for detail, said she wanted to discuss an important piece of evidence they had not yet gone over. "We haven't discussed the fibers found on the victim's clothing yet. The prosecution said they matched the unique type of jacket the defendant owned. And the only store in the state that sells this is just a block from his house. That's pretty solid, don't you think?"

The jurors nodded in agreement, murmuring among themselves. Robert felt a familiar surge of anxiety. He knew this piece of evidence all too well, recalling how he likely brushed against the victim during the struggle. He had to be careful, yet he needed to cast doubt on this evidence without revealing the source of his knowledge.

Robert leaned forward, his expression thoughtful. "Let's think about those fibers for a moment. Sure, they matched the type of jacket the defendant owns, but how unique is it, really? Just because there's only one store in the state that sells it doesn't mean it's unique and that the defendant could be the only source of those fibers."

Alice looked skeptical. "But it's still quite a coincidence, don't you think? His fibers were found on the victim, and there is only one store in the state that sells it – right by his place? Using credit card receipts, they tracked down all but one of the other people who purchased those jackets, and they all had alibis. The one they didn't track down might have been purchased with cash, but the owner of the store testified that, after reviewing his books, it's far more likely this is an inventory error – that the only jackets sold were those that were purchased with credit cards, including the one purchased by the defendant. And there were only, at most, seven sold by that store. This evidence really narrows things down to the defendant, don't you think?"

"True," Robert conceded, "but let's dig deeper. I actually lived out of state for many years, and there was a store there that sold that exact same jacket. I remember this because I bought one."

As soon as the words left his mouth, a wave of fear crashed over him. His heart pounded, and his palms grew clammy. He had just admitted to owning the same type of jacket, a detail that could easily tie him to the crime. His mind raced with the implications, each scenario worse than the last. He tried to keep his expression neutral, scanning the faces of his fellow jurors. Relief washed over him as he saw their expressions – thoughtful, contemplative, but not suspicious. No one seemed to have made the connection. The only person he couldn't see was Amara, her face obscured by Caroline, who was leaning forward in deep concentration.

The uncertainty weighed on him, but for now, it seemed that he had dodged a bullet. Robert always regretted buying that jacket. After today he disliked it even more.

"So, it's not impossible for those fibers to come from someone else who owned a similar jacket, even if they didn't buy it from that specific store near the defendant's house. This evidence doesn't narrow things down as much as the prosecutor would like you to believe. We have no idea how many people in this area own one of those jackets. The fibers could have come from someone other than the defendant. No one mentioned anything about whether it's available for purchase online. I'm not saying that it is. The point is, we can't conclude that the jacket is unique enough to conclusively tie the defendant to the scene."

Amara, visibly frustrated, cut in. "There you go again, Robert, flipping the script! It's always some excuse with you. We can't keep second-guessin' every single piece of evidence!" As she spoke, her eyes lingered on Robert, a hint of suspicion creeping into her gaze. Robert noticed the subtle change in her demeanor and it seemed clear that she was now starting to question his motives. He shifted uncomfortably in his seat, hoping his facade remained intact despite her penetrating scrutiny.

Caroline, ever the voice of reason, interjected calmly. "Now, Amara, he's raising valid points. We need to scrutinize every piece of evidence with the same critical eye. If there's reasonable doubt, we can't be just brushing it aside."

The foreperson nodded, reinforcing the point. "Caroline is right. We can't afford to overlook any plausible explanations. We're here to ensure justice is served, and that means questioning everything thoroughly."

It was at this point that Robert really noticed Caroline. She was slender and tall, with a kind and beautiful face that seemed to radiate grace and an almost royal bearing. Her every movement was graceful, hinting at an upbringing that valued poise and elegance. Yet, occasionally, there were brief signs in her eyes, or a fleeting expression, that hinted at a deep sadness she had experienced in her life. Perhaps multiple experiences of sadness.

Her appearance was a contradiction. She looked like she came from money, her clothes and demeanor suggesting a background of privilege. However, there were subtle clues that she might not have as much now. Despite this, she definitely didn't look like she went without anything, maintaining an air of composure and self-assuredness. This blend of apparent wealth and hints of hardship made her a bit of a mystery, intriguing Robert even more.

Robert's attention was drawn back to the room as the foreperson glanced around, sensing the growing tension and the need to gauge where everyone stood after their lengthy discussions. Clearing his throat, he addressed the group, "I know we haven't gone over all the evidence yet as a group, but I believe it might be a good time to take another vote. After all, we started with everyone voting guilty. Let's see if that's even changed."

The jurors exchanged looks, some nodding in agreement, others appearing hesitant. Amara essentially ended the uncertainty. "Fine, but no more secrecy. Let's do a roll call."

The foreperson nodded and picked up his pen and a notepad, preparing to record each juror's vote. He decided to conduct the roll call by juror number, to ensure he didn't miss anyone.

"Juror 1," he began, looking at the first juror.
"Not guilty," came the reply from Blake.

"Juror 2?"
"Not guilty."

"Juror 3?"
"Not guilty," replied Caroline. The

foreperson continued down the line, each juror responding in turn.

> "Juror 4?"
> "Not guilty."
>
> "Juror 5?"
> "Not guilty."
>
> "Juror 6?"
> "Not guilty."
>
> "Juror 7?"

"Guilty," Amara said firmly, her voice carrying a weight of conviction. The room shifted slightly as everyone processed her vote. The foreperson moved on.

> "Juror 9?"
> "Not guilty."
>
> "Juror 10?"
> "Not guilty."
>
> "Juror 11?"
> "Definitely guilty," replied John insistently.

Robert felt a knot in his stomach tighten as the votes were being called out. The foreperson looked up and stared at Robert.

> "Juror 12?"

"Not guilty," Robert answered, his voice steady despite the inner turmoil.

"As the jury foreperson, Juror 8, I cast my vote as guilty."

The foreperson reviewed his notes and looked up. "That's three votes for guilty, and the rest for not guilty. We clearly still have a lot to discuss."

Amara mumbled to herself, "Now look what you've gone and done." It was a clear reference to Robert.

Robert realized that even though there were only three jurors left who believed the defendant was guilty, the task of convincing all three seemed insurmountable. The remaining jurors were entrenched in their positions, their convictions bolstered by a combination of personal experiences, biases, and interpretations of the evidence, with Amara providing strong support for the other two. With each passing hour of deliberation, it became increasingly clear to Robert that swaying their opinions would require a herculean effort, one that he wasn't sure he was capable of.

As he glanced at Amara, a sense of resignation washed over him. She had been particularly vocal in her belief that the defendant was guilty. Despite presenting evidence and engaging in reasoned debate, Amara remained resolute in her conviction of the defendant's guilt. Her unwavering stance puzzled Robert, as he struggled to understand the source of her steadfast belief. It seemed as though Amara's motives for persistently arguing for guilt were elusive, shrouded in mystery.

As Robert considered the prospect of trying to sway Amara's opinion, a sense of frustration and resignation settled over him. It appeared increasingly unlikely that he would be able to overcome her steadfast resistance and achieve the unanimity necessary for a verdict. Robert's eyes flickered to Amara, who met his gaze with a resolute expression.

The weight of their continued deliberations loomed large, but for now, at least, the majority leaned towards acquittal. The room settled into a contemplative silence once more. Robert could feel the tension easing slightly as his fellow jurors reconsidered their original votes.

He knew the truth behind his arguments, rooted in his own actions and intimate knowledge of the crime scene. With every piece of evidence he questioned, he hoped they would be a step closer to ensuring the right verdict – one that would keep an innocent man from paying for his sin. The certainty of guilt that once seemed so solid was now beginning to erode, piece by piece.

And as he reflected on his own slip about the jacket, he realized how close he had come to revealing his secret, yet no one seemed to have caught on. But the precarious edge that Robert momentarily found himself on seemed foretelling of the entire deliberations. Then he reminded himself of his difficult task ahead, with three determined guilty votes.

The foreperson then announced, "I think we should take a one-hour break to clear our heads and take some time to gather our thoughts. I know it's a bit longer than usual, but we need to come back fresh and ready to dig deeper into this case."

CHAPTER 8

Racism

As the jurors trickled back into the room from their one-hour break, the tension was palpable. It appeared the break didn't settle anyone down. The foreperson cleared his throat to get everyone's attention. "Alright, let's settle back in and resume our deliberations."

Amidst the intensity of their deliberations, the room oscillated between tense silence and bursts of animated conversation. Chester, a retired veteran, occasionally interjected with anecdotes from his past experiences, attempting to inject levity into the proceedings. However, his stories were met with polite nods rather than rapt attention, as the other jurors remained focused on the task at hand. John, a diligent, recent college graduate, occasionally sought clarification on legal matters, his earnest inquiries serving to keep the discussions grounded in reality.

Meanwhile, Blake, the youngest member of the panel, often found himself struggling to keep up with the complexities of the case. Though he attempted to participate in the discussions, his contributions were tentative and often misguided, reflecting his uncertainty about the legal process. Occasionally, Blake would make offhand remarks about Amara, though these comments seemed to stem more from ignorance than malice. Despite attempts to redirect the focus back to the evidence, Blake's persistent confusion continued to punctuate the deliberations, creating an uneasy atmosphere in the room.

Blake, seemingly anxious to say something, shifted in his seat and spoke. "You know, I was thinking about this during the break, and it still rings true to me. I think Amara is biased. She's not looking at the evidence fairly."

Amara shot a sharp look at Blake, but before she could say anything, Caroline intervened on her side. "Well, now, that ain't fair, Blake. We're all examining the evidence in our own way, with our own experiences."

Amara seized the moment. "I'm checking out the evidence just like you, Blake. Maybe it's time you check your privilege at the door, honey."

Blake's face reddened. "No, listen. I'm just sayin'. I mean, maybe you've got some, I don't know, personal issues clouding your judgment."

Amara's expression hardened. "Personal

issues? That's a low blow. We here to find the truth, not be throwing shade at each other."

Blake's frustration boiled over as he turned to the foreperson, as if he was speaking only to him. "I'm not trying to be rude, but some people just don't understand how the system works, you know. Like maybe they come from places where the law doesn't mean as much." Then he turned to Amara, "Let's face it, sometimes you people just don't get it, that's all. I'm just sayin' what's true."

Amara's silence spoke volumes, her eyes blazing with restrained fury and indignation. Seeing the escalating situation, the foreperson raised his hands. "Alright, that's enough. We're clearly not in the right mindset to continue today. I'm recessing the deliberations until tomorrow morning at 9:00 AM. Let's come back with clear heads and we'll continue deliberations then."

Realizing he had crossed a line, Blake's face softened and he quickly began to speak before everyone could leave. "I … I'm sorry. That was out of line. I didn't mean it like that." But it seemed to fall on deaf ears. The jurors began to file out of the room, the charged atmosphere lingering as they left for the day.

CHAPTER 9

Robert's Secret Revealed?

The jury assembled promptly in the deliberation room, each member taking their seat in a somber and focused manner. Unlike the previous morning, there was a notable absence of casual discussions or small talk. The weight of their responsibility seemed to hang in the air, a silent acknowledgment of the grave importance of their task.

The foreperson officially called the deliberations to order, marking the beginning of what would be a thorough examination of the remaining pieces of evidence. This morning's deliberations were characterized by a meticulous and methodical review. While these pieces of evidence were reviewed with the same level of scrutiny as those discussed previously, it quickly became evident that, while they were consequential, these pieces of evidence were still less important to the case overall.

The jurors engaged in detailed analysis, to ensure that every aspect was considered, but there was a collective sense that these pieces did not carry the same weight as the critical evidence already discussed. Despite the lower significance, the jury maintained their diligence, respecting the process and the necessity of a comprehensive review. It was a testament to the jury system.

The discussion continued without interruption throughout the morning, a reflection of the jury's commitment and focus. They refrained from taking breaks, fully engrossed in their task, driven by a shared sense of purpose, duty, and justice.

As the morning deliberations concluded, the foreperson announced a one-and-a-half-hour lunch break. This decision was met with a mixture of relief and understanding. The break was necessary, providing the jurors with a much-needed opportunity to rest and recoup before resuming their critical discussions in the afternoon.

During the lunch break, Caroline approached Robert, her steps deliberate yet casual. Robert had been unusually quiet throughout the morning deliberations, and her curiosity about this got the better of her.

"Hey, I noticed you didn't say much this mornin'. Are you alright, sugah?" Her tone was friendly with a hint of concern.

Robert looked up, offering a small smile that could be interpreted in many ways. "Yeah, I'm fine. Just ... different thoughts running through my head, I guess."

Caroline tilted her head slightly, a glimmer of something almost playful in her eyes. "Different thoughts? Care to share, darlin'?"

He sighed, leaning back a bit as he gathered his thoughts. "Overnight, I realized I don't need to be so active in the discussions anymore. The majority of us are leaning towards not guilty. The big pieces of evidence are already out of the way, there's nothing major left to sway anyone with."

She nodded, prompting him to continue.

"Basically, I've accomplished what I set out to do. My goal was to prevent a man I know is innocent from being found guilty."

"You *know* he's innocent? How do you know that?"

"No, I didn't mean it that way. The evidence doesn't add up to guilt. And with the way things are going, it looks like it could end up a hung jury at worst or, at best, maybe an acquittal."

Caroline gave him a thoughtful look, the hint of a smile playing on her red lips. "So, you're just gonna sit back and let things unfold, sugah?"

Robert shrugged lightly. "Pretty much. I mean, you won't understand this, but I'm terrified of what I might say. As long as things stay on course, we're probably heading for an acquittal. And that's what matters to me – making sure we don't convict an innocent man."

She seemed to consider this for a moment, seemingly curious about his certainty of the man's innocence. "Well, I'm glad you're OK. Just wanted to check in, hon." Her tone was light, but there was a subtle undercurrent, almost as if she were trying to read more into his words and demeanor.

"Thanks," he replied, his smile returning. "I appreciate it."

With that, the two jurors parted ways, each reflecting on the conversation in their own way as they prepared to resume the afternoon session. The brief interaction added a layer of complexity to their dynamic, leaving room for interpretation and speculation.

The jurors returned to their seats after the lunch break, resuming their positions around the deliberation table. The foreperson once again called the session to order, and for the next two hours the discussions continued in the same manner as they had in the morning. The jurors reviewed the remaining evidence, finding it less consequential but still giving it due consideration.

Then there was an unexpected pivotal moment when the foreperson began to speak. "Throughout the trial, I was certain our job was simply to determine whether the defendant was guilty or innocent," the foreperson began, his voice measured. "By the time the trial concluded, I was convinced of the defendant's guilt. But since we've begun our deliberations, my perspective has shifted."

He paused, allowing his words to sink in before continuing. "I now understand that our responsibility is to examine the evidence meticulously. We must scrutinize everything presented by both the prosecution and defense. And that's what we've been doing. Regardless of our personal beliefs, we must follow the evidence. But even as we go over these smaller pieces of evidence I've come to know how I should be voting. Based on the scrutiny we've applied, I'm no longer convinced of the defendant's guilt."

His statement hung in the air, the significance of his words palpable. "Look, my gut tells me one thing, and that's what's been holding me back from changing my vote. But I can't deny the evidence, which says something else. I still think he's guilty but there's clearly substantial room for reasonable doubt," he concluded, his expression troubled. "So, I'm changing my vote to not guilty."

"The foreperson's right," John interjected firmly. "I've been wrestling with the same doubts."

John leaned forward with a look of concentration. "You know, I've been thinking about this a lot," he began, his voice steady but contemplative. "When we first started, I was convinced. The prosecution's case seemed airtight. But the more we've gone over the evidence, the more holes I've seen."

He paused, glancing around the room to gauge the reactions of his fellow jurors. "Take the lack of conclusive physical evidence placing the defendant at the scene of the crime, for example. They couldn't find the murder weapon! That's a big deal, don't you think? How can we convict someone when there's no direct link tying them to the commission of the crime?"

Robert nodded, his eyes focused on John. The room was quiet, each juror processing John's words.

"And then there are the witnesses," John continued. "The neighbor's testimony was shaky at best. She admitted she couldn't see clearly."

John took a deep breath, his resolve strengthening. "We also need to consider the timeline. The prosecution's theory doesn't fit neatly with the sequence of events. There are gaps, moments that just don't add up. It's like witnesses were viewing the defendant at different times – or two different people committed the crime. We can't fill those gaps with assumptions."

He leaned back in his chair, looking at each juror in turn. "Reasonable doubt isn't just a technicality. It's the cornerstone of our justice system. If we have any doubt about Daniel's guilt, we can't in good conscience convict him. It's our duty to ensure that we're making the right decision, not just the easy one."

The room remained silent as John's words hung in the air. His reasoning, methodical and clear, seemed to resonate with the jurors. They all had been grappling with their own similar doubts and uncertainties, and John's articulate expression of those doubts brought a sense of clarity to the deliberations.

John concluded, "We have to be absolutely certain, beyond a shadow of a doubt, before we can take away someone's freedom. And right now, I just don't see how we can be certain. That's why I'm changing my vote to not guilty."

The foreperson nodded, acknowledging John's thoughtful contribution. "Thank you, John. It's important that we all share our perspectives and doubts. This decision carries a lot of weight, and we need to make sure we get it right."

The jurors, absorbing John's reasoning, seemed to reflect intently on their own positions, the weight of their responsibility pressing heavily on their minds.

Then Amara stood up, her frustration evident in her eyes. "I can't believe this," she said, her voice shaking with emotion. "An open and shut case, and now y'all are ready to let a guilty man walk free? How can you be so blind to the facts? This is ridiculous! And it's all because of you, Robert. You started this mess!"

Robert remained seated, his face calm and composed. "Amara, I understand you're upset," he said gently. "But we're here to ensure justice is served. We have to consider every piece of evidence carefully. It's not about letting someone walk free; it's about making sure we don't convict an innocent man. We have to be certain."

Amara crossed her arms, her expression hardening. "Oh, don't give me that," she shot back. "I've seen you play devil's advocate from the start, sowing seeds of doubt. But the evidence is clear! The prosecutor laid it all out. We can't just ignore that."

Robert nodded slowly, choosing his words with care. "I'm not ignoring the evidence, Amara. But reasonable doubt exists, and it's our duty to address it. If there's any reasonable chance that Daniel didn't commit this crime, we owe it to him and ourselves to consider it."

Caroline, sensing the escalating tension, stepped in, her voice soothing but firm with her Southern drawl. "Amara, Robert, let's take a step back," she said. "We're all on the same side here. We all want justice. We need to listen to each other and weigh everything carefully. Let's not turn this into a battle. We need to remain calm and focused on our duty. There's nothing wrong with Amara holding to her view on this case."

Amara glanced at Caroline, her anger dimming slightly but still evident. She took a deep breath and sat down, her arms still crossed. The room fell into a heavy silence, the weight of their task pressing down on them.

The foreperson cleared his throat, breaking the silence. "We need to stay objective and thorough," he said. "Let's take a moment to gather our thoughts and then continue reviewing the evidence. We have a responsibility to get this right."

The jurors, chastened by the exchange, sat

quietly, each lost in their own thoughts. The tension lingered, but Caroline's intervention had restored a semblance of calm, allowing them to refocus on their deliberations.

Robert thought to himself how he was now closer to a not-guilty verdict. The only guilty vote that remained was Amara's. At first he wasn't sure if John and the foreperson would change their votes, but they did. With only one guilty vote left, victory was almost assured. He knew from his days in law enforcement that it was difficult, if not impossible, for just one juror to hold out against the rest. Lone holdouts often needed one or two others to give them the support they needed. But even if Amara refused to change her vote, she wasn't going to sway the jury back to guilty. It was done. There were only two outcomes now: acquittal or a hung jury. And to Robert's great relief, that meant he didn't have to confess.

Just as Robert finished processing this, Amara spoke. "Robert," she began, her tone measured and firm, "I know what you thinkin', but you don't want the rest of us to know."

Robert felt a sudden pang of anxiety. Could she have figured out he was the murderer? No. He tried to keep his composure, though his heart raced. "What do you mean?" he replied, his voice steady but with an edge of tension. Everyone's eyes moved towards Amara.

"I know you think you've won," she said, her eyes locking onto his.

He felt a wave of relief wash over him. She was a smart woman, she obviously came to the same conclusion he had about a guilty verdict being beyond reach now. But his curiosity was still piqued by why she would raise this with him. "What do you mean by that?"

Amara leaned forward slightly, "You think a hung jury is a win for you. But it's not. A hung jury means another trial. Another trial means another jury. And another jury means one without you on it to twist things around. That means a hung jury at this trial means guilty at the next. And I ain't never changing my vote, Mista Robert."

The implications of her words sank in slowly for Robert. As the horror of her statement dawned on him, he realized she was right. He had been so focused on simply preventing a guilty verdict now and accepting a hung jury that he hadn't considered the possibility of what another jury might conclude without his influence.

Robert thought he could escape a confession. But he realized Amara meant what she said; she was never going to change her vote to not guilty. He tried, but it was over. He couldn't let an innocent man go to jail, which was what would likely happen after an acquittal in this trail. At a minimum, the risk of this outcome was too high. Robert realized he had a duty to confess.

Robert said, with barely more than a whisper, "I have a confession to make."

Amara looked over at him with a stone-cold

glaze. She had been skeptical of Robert throughout deliberations. Now she looked vindicated, like she knew exactly what Robert was going to say.

Before Robert could say anything more, the foreperson, clearly seeing that everyone's patience was nearing its end, intervened. "Alright, that's enough for today. We're nearly done for today anyways. Let's end the deliberations and return at the same time tomorrow."

The jurors slowly began to gather their things, the room buzzing with the unresolved tension from Amara's commitment to voting guilty. Robert couldn't shake the feeling of dread that had settled in his gut, but he also appreciated he was going to have a moment to reflect on how to assemble the words of his confession.

CHAPTER 10

The Realization

Robert usually drove straight home after the day's deliberations, but not today. He had always known this might end with him confessing, even though he had come so close to avoiding it.

With no desire to cook or eat at home, Robert decided to go to his favorite diner instead. The familiar comfort of the place would offer a brief escape from his turmoil. He walked into the cozy, dimly lit spot, greeted by the scent of sizzling burgers and fresh coffee. The walls were covered with vintage photos from around town, and the hum of quiet conversations created a soothing backdrop.

As Robert entered, he spotted two detectives sitting at a booth near the back, complaining about the end of a long day. The diner was a popular hangout for law enforcement, and seeing his colleagues there always helped Robert feel a bit more at ease.

He slid into a booth near the window, the leather seat creaking under his weight. The waitress, a middle-aged woman with a kind smile, approached him. "Evening, Robert. The usual?"

"Yes, please," Robert replied, his voice lacking its usual enthusiasm. As she turned to leave, he added, "And a glass of the house red. Just one, I'm driving."

"Sure thing, hon," she said with a nod.

While he waited, Robert gazed out the window, watching the traffic lights change and cars pass by. The waitress soon returned with his wine and a basket of warm, crusty bread. He took a sip, savoring the rich flavor, and broke off a piece of bread. As he chewed, his thoughts drifted to the consequences that would follow his confession.

The two detectives in the diner were only a couple of tables away, their conversation carrying over the quiet hum of the place. Robert's attention shifted to them as they talked, their voices low but clear enough for him to catch snippets.

"This was one of my toughest days. It just keeps getting tougher," one detective said, shaking his head. "More complex cases, less training. We're not equipped for it all."

His partner nodded, taking a sip of his coffee. "Tell me about it. I can't be an expert in everything — addiction, mental health, poverty. It's too much. Captain said the top brass can't get more funding for training. Pfft."

Robert nodded subtly, understanding their frustration. He remembered the same battles he had fought for funding when he was a captain. He had been there, faced those same challenges. The job demanded more than just enforcing the law; it required empathy, understanding, and constantly evolving skills that needed more training than most police departments provided.

The waitress brought his main meal, steaming and fragrant. He took his time eating it, but barely noticing the taste as his mind was consumed with his decision – and the conversation of the two detectives. He listened, feeling a pang of nostalgia for the camaraderie and the shared sense of purpose he had once known.

"Yeah," the first detective continued, "Frank's quitting." The second detective seemed shocked. "His wife got a promotion. So he said he doesn't need the hassle. Going to the private sector: consulting and security."

Robert took another sip of his wine, feeling the weight of their words. He had loved the job too, despite its hardships. But now, his love for justice had driven him to a crossroads he couldn't ignore.

As he finished his meal, the detectives paid their bill and left, their conversation lingering in Robert's mind. He felt a kinship with them, a shared understanding of the burdens they carried. And as he sat there, finishing his wine, he resolved to face his own burden head-on, knowing that the path to redemption was fraught with uncertainty but driven by a deep, unyielding sense of duty.

The waitress returned to clear the table, her experienced movements quick and efficient. "Room for dessert?" she asked.

He hesitated, then nodded. "Yes, please. The coconut cream pie, if you have any left."

She smiled, nodded, and disappeared into the kitchen, returning moments later with a generous slice of pie. Robert ate slowly, trying to savor each bite, but his thoughts were elsewhere.

After finishing his dessert, Robert paid the bill and left the diner. The night air was cool and it refreshingly hit his face as he stepped outside and looked around. The streets were quiet, the world moving on as if nothing had changed. Yet for Robert, everything had. He walked to his car, each step feeling heavier than the last, then he took the long way home, almost as if by dragging out his routine he could drag out time itself and put off the confession.

◆ ◆ ◆

When he got home, he went straight to the attic. Going to that diner made him reminisce, and he wanted to go down memory lane some more. The attic was a dimly lit, musty space, filled with the scent of aged wood and moist cardboard. Specks of dust floated lazily in the last beams of sunlight of the day that filtered through the two small, grimy windows. He pulled the light on and then pulled out a couple of boxes that stored items from his days on the force. One by one, he went through them.

There was his first badge, gleaming under the dust, a symbol of his early dreams and ambitions. He traced his fingers over the engraved number, remembering the pride he felt pinning it to his uniform for the first time. Next, he found a stack of commendation letters, their crisp edges softened by time. Each one represented a moment of valor, a life saved, a criminal apprehended. As he read through them, his chest tightened with a mix of pride and sorrow.

Then there was his old service revolver, no longer functional but still heavy with memories. It lay nestled in its case, a silent testament to the countless times it had been drawn in the line of duty. He picked it up, feeling the cold metal against his skin, and remembered the split-second decisions that had defined his career.

Finally, he came across a faded photograph of his old squad. They stood together, arms around each other, grinning after a tough case. The camaraderie, the shared sense of purpose — they were all captured in that single, timeless moment.

He sat back, surrounded by the artifacts of his past, and let out a deep breath. The attic was quiet, save for a faint creaking every once in a while. He realized that all of his accomplishments would now be tarnished by the murder. A wave of bittersweet emotions washed over him. Each item was a piece of his past, a reminder of who he was and the choices he had made. But now, every photo, every commendation, every memory would be overshadowed by that one fateful choice. The sense of pride he once felt now seemed hollow, replaced by a burning sense of guilt. Robert decided to go to sleep early and to put everything away in the morning.

❖ ❖ ❖

Robert woke remarkably refreshed. Yesterday's guilt had been replaced with newfound determination. It seemed he had decided that confession was something he always needed to do. He made his breakfast, drank his coffee. As he walked around his house it was with a sense of purpose. His normally composed demeanor was replaced by a restless energy, evident in the tense set of his shoulders.

The day was starting out very well. Once Robert placed the dishes in the dishwasher, he went up to the attic to pack away the boxes. The two windows caught the morning's brightness and lit up the room. Robert quickly stuffed everything back into the boxes and carried them away. But clearly, he was walking a little too quickly. A newspaper clipping whisked out of one of the boxes and floated for a moment, hanging lazily in the air, as if making sure its presence was known before settling softly on the floor.

Robert picked up the clipping. It was about one of his most prized investigations. This crime had been solved with good old-fashioned detective work, and it was hard. At trial, the defendant's lawyer tried to make a case that his client was framed by the police. And he did a good job at it, too. There were some mistakes the police made that the defendant tried to twist around. But there's always something that can be painted as less than perfect. They hadn't done anything wrong.

Then it hit Robert. He had the benefit of all of his years of experience to make sure that after the murder he committed he left no evidence behind that pointed back to him. He also left some clues to throw investigators off his track. But now he realized the implications of this. Now every single person he helped convict would argue that Robert was a bad cop who destroyed and planted evidence – and they would claim that because he did. Every single person he helped convict who was still in prison would have grounds to file an appeal, and maybe get off, because of how he covered up his own crime by destroying and planting evidence.

Who would have thought you could get hit by a wrecking ball twice in the same month?

CHAPTER 11

The Confrontation

Robert arrived at the courthouse early that morning. As the early morning light filtered through the windows of the jury room, Robert had to decide what he was to do. He could think of nothing else since the conundrum first entered his head that morning. He could confess, and potentially several guilty criminals could walk free because the evidence their convictions were built upon would now be cast in doubt. Or, he could let one innocent man go to jail – the defendant in this trial. Technically, of course, he knew there was one other option, as far-fetched as that option might seem: convince Amara to change her vote.

Robert looked over to Amara. She and Caroline were exchanging words – and laughter. It wasn't unusual to see the two of them talking it up at the courthouse. They hit it off right from orientation on. Then he heard the foreperson.

"Please, everyone, take your seats and let's begin."

"I do believe Robert started something last night that he was unable to finish," Amara quickly stated.

Robert quickly replied, "Oh it wasn't important. I just wanted to say that I must confess this has been a much more difficult task than I had expected. I'm sure others feel the same way and I want to thank them all for their work."

Amara replied, her voice low but firm. "Oh, Robert, don't think I don't know you're hidin' something. Your lil' friend is catching on too. But she doesn't have the same instincts I do. I don't just know you're hidin' something, I know what it is, too."

Maybe Caroline should have been a little offended. But she was too consumed by it all. She popped to attention and gave a curious look, first to Robert, then to Amara. The air in the room grew thick with unspoken questions and suspicions.

As the weight of what Amara had just said settled over the room, all eyes turned expectantly towards Robert. Robert addressed Amara with a calm yet firm tone, his words carrying the weight of anticipation that had been building in the room.

"Amara," he began, his voice steady, "if what you believe I'm hiding has nothing to do with the trial at hand, then perhaps we should set it aside for now. But if it's relevant to this case, then I believe you owe it to everyone here to put it on the table."

He paused, allowing his words to sink in, before continuing, "We're here to ensure justice is served, and if there's any information pertinent to our deliberations, we need to address it openly and honestly."

Robert believed in ensuring justice was served; his whole career was based on that. But even as he said the words, he wasn't so sure if he wanted Amara to be open and honest. Though he had done everything to avoid being caught for his crime, he was now personally prepared to suffer the consequences of his actions. He always was; he just hoped he could avoid them. But our actions are like stones cast into still water. They create ripples that emanate out from the center. The effects of our actions disperse, sometimes farther and in ways we do not always anticipate.

Robert had not fully considered the consequences of his actions. He understood them now, though. And while he was prepared to suffer for his choice, he did not want guilty men to walk free because of his decisions. He knew the way out of this: convince Amara. But he seemed to have neither the time nor the ability to accomplish that. He was in dire need of help right now – divine help if necessary.

At that moment, the lights went off in the deliberation room. At first, everyone sat quietly, thinking the power might come right back on. Then, as moments passed, they sat in uncertain silence, unsure of what to do next. Should they continue? A few people got up and peered out the windows while others murmured at the table. The atmosphere grew tense.

The bailiff entered the room and informed the jury that the power was out on the whole block. There was planned electrical work being undertaken on their block. A mistake happened and the crew expected it to be restored quickly but didn't know exactly how long it would take.

The foreperson decided to announce a break in deliberations.

Robert retreated to a window in the corner of the room, as if the answer to his current dilemma could be found by looking outside. He stared at the street below, searching for a way out of the tangled web he found himself in.

Caroline approached him, her accent breaking the silence. "Hey there, sugah. Mind if we have a li'l chat?" she asked, her tone casual yet tinged with concern.

Robert nodded, curious about what she wanted to discuss. He had come to look forward to hearing the musical quality of her Southern accent, no matter what she said. "Sure, what's on your mind?" he replied, his voice friendly.

"I don't think any of us can miss how you and Amara like to tango," Caroline began, her gaze steady. "You two are like two roosters in a henhouse. I get that you two have your differences, but maybe you could cut her some slack?"

Robert sighed, running a hand through his hair, fully aware of how he wanted to confront Amara. "I respect her, I really do," he admitted. "But it's hard to avoid the conflict when she seems to thrive on it with me."

Caroline nodded in understanding, but then she looked at Robert with curiosity, her eyes sparkling with warmth. "You know, I've been meaning to ask you somethin'," she said, her voice thoughtful. "Why do you think Amara and I get along so well?"

Robert raised an eyebrow, surprised by her question. "Honestly, I've been wondering about that," he replied, his interest piqued.

Caroline took a deep breath, considering her words carefully. "Well, I reckon it's because I look for the good in people. And I look for what I have in common with 'em. Amara and I aren't all that different," she explained. "I mean, from the outside, it might seem like we come from different worlds, but we actually have a lot in common."

Robert listened intently, absorbing her words. His mind wandered as he contemplated her perspective of looking for what you have in common with someone, considering his own experiences on the force and the connections he might find with Amara based on those experiences.

Caroline continued, her voice tinged with empathy, a trait that seemed to help define who she was. "I grew up in the South, surrounded by Black culture. I had a Black nanny that I still love, and in the South I couldn't avoid being immersed in parts of their way of life – the food, the music, the stories …"

Robert interjected, with a tone of authority. "Now you're sounding naive."

"Oh sugah, I may not be good with words like you, but I'm anythin' but naive. I understand that despite those connections, I likely never faced the hardships Amara has," she acknowledged softly. "Even with what we share, her struggles and experiences are her own, and they run deep and define her in ways that I just can't ever understand."

She paused for a moment, then added, "You know, maybe saying we're alike in some ways is just the wrong way to describe it. Like I said, I'm not good with words, Robert. Maybe the better way is to say that the two of us have built bridges to each other based on common experiences. When you've seen her and I having a hoot as we talk to each other, we've been building bridges. It's those bridges that we've built that we share, and sugah, her and I do love spending time together on those bridges."

Then she looked Robert straight in his eyes, "And maybe if you tried real hard, you could build a bridge and make that connection with her too. I know you've seen a lot as a police officer, Robert. You've dealt with people from all walks of life, faced the complexities of human behavior, seen the good and bad of what people are capable of. You might have to build the whole bridge on your own, but there's room to build one to her if you're willing to build it."

Robert nodded slowly, her words resonating with him. She had a way of reaching him that others didn't. Reflecting on his time in law enforcement, he realized that he and Amara might share a common understanding of justice and the complexities of human behavior. He had witnessed the discrimination that people of color faced. He couldn't fathom how Blacks endured so much discrimination. And he never turned a blind eye to it, either. Despite their obvious differences, perhaps they both shared a genuine sense of duty and a desire to see justice served. Maybe he could build a bridge to her on those grounds.

Robert turned to Caroline, his voice tinged with a newfound determination. "You know, Caroline, I've seen a lot in my years on the force. I've seen good people go through hell because of the color of their skin. I've seen the system fail them, time and time again. I've always believed that, deep down, justice has to mean something. It has to be fair, or it's not justice at all."

Caroline looked at him, her eyes softening. "I reckon you and Amara might have more in common than you think, Robert. She's all about justice too, and she's got a good heart. Maybe if you talked to her, really talked to her, you could find some common ground to build that bridge."

Robert turned back to the window, the street below still shrouded in darkness, but his path forward began to clear. Robert sighed, the weight of his predicament still heavy on his shoulders, and not able to fully tell Caroline what he was struggling with. "You're right. I need to find a way to reach Amara. That's my only choice."

Caroline nodded, her expression encouraging. "Speak from your heart; show her that you mean it, and you might break through. But listen to her too, Robert. The conversation can't just be about what you want to say to her."

Robert and Caroline were so caught up in their thoughts and conversation that they hadn't noticed the lights had come back on in the room. The foreperson called out, "Alright, everyone, please take your seats. We can resume deliberations." Robert and Caroline exchanged a final glance before joining the others at the table, both pondering the bridges they might yet build.

Once they all sat down, Amara leaned forward, her voice carrying the echoes of her upbringing as she addressed Robert. "Robert," she began, her tone tinged with frustration, "seems to me like you don't wanna hear what I gotta say. What I know ain't somethin' you wanna hear 'bout. It's somethin' you been hidin' from."

Her words pierced Robert, unsettling him as he grappled with the implications of her accusation. Perhaps he was wrong. Perhaps there was a fourth option for him today: to be exposed by Amara. He shifted uneasily in his seat, feeling the weight of her stare bearing down on him. "It just might be that I've been hiding from something," he admitted, his voice tinged with apprehension. "But I'm ready to hear it."

As Robert spoke, the room fell into a tense silence, with all eyes fixed on Amara, hanging on her every word. Her words had sparked a collective anticipation, each juror eager to uncover the truth behind her accusation.

Amara leaned forward, her eyes narrowing as she fixed a penetrating gaze on Robert. "Listen here, Robert," she began, her voice carrying a subtle edge of accusation. "I been watchin' you, see? You twistin' and turnin' every which way, like a snake in the grass."

Her words hung in the air, heavy with implication, as the other jurors exchanged uncertain glances. Yet, beneath the surface, there lingered a second meaning, a whispered insinuation that hinted at a deeper truth waiting to be uncovered.

"Now, I ain't one to point fingers," Amara continued, her tone carefully measured. "But it don't take a genius to see what's goin' on here. You think you're pullin' the wool over our eyes, but I ain't buyin' it."

As her words reverberated through the room, a sense of unease settled over the jurors, each one grappling with the implications of Amara's cryptic accusations. Yet, amidst the tension, a flicker of understanding danced in some eyes, as they began to decipher the hidden meaning behind her pointed words.

Robert absorbed Amara's words, his

expression a mix of confusion and concern. The accusation hung heavy in the air, and he felt a knot form in the pit of his stomach. As the other jurors exchanged uneasy glances, Robert couldn't shake the feeling that there was more to her statement than met the eye. All he knew was that the atmosphere in the room had shifted, and the weight of suspicion now hung heavily over him. With a sense of unease gnawing at him, Robert couldn't help but wonder if Amara had inadvertently stumbled upon the truth — or if his own guilt was merely playing tricks on his mind.

Amara fixed her gaze on Robert, her expression a mix of anger and resignation. "You're just like most cops I've met," she began, her voice carrying the weight of a lifetime's worth of experiences. "Y'all treat white folks with respect, but when it comes to Black folks — especially Black men — we're instantly seen as dangers that need to be feared."

As she spoke, her gaze turned distant, transported back to individual moments of prejudice. Then, delving into personal anecdotes, she recounted the harsh realities of racial bias that transcended the encounters she had with law enforcement. "I remember one time as a young girl," she began, her voice tinged with bitterness. "We were in a high-end store, just lookin' at some clothes. Ma won some money at bingo and wanted to buy somethin' nice for once." The memory seemed to unfold before her eyes. "This white lady, she was all smiles and friendly with everyone else, but soon as we walked in, she started tailin' us, like we were gonna steal somethin'. Every step we took, there she was, watchin' us like a hawk."

Her voice gained intensity as she recounted another painful memory. "And then there was the first time a boy took me out for dinner at a nice restaurant. We sat down, ready to enjoy our meal, but the waiter took forever to serve us. Gave us these looks, like we didn't belong there. Took our order last, brought our food out cold." The injustice of the moment was palpable. "We hadn't done nuttin' wrong, just wanted to have a nice evening out. And then the waiter explains to us how to use the machine to pay with our credit card, how to enter the tip, like we were idiots incapable of understanding modern technology. Even fools like us can figure out a zero percent tip, thank you very much!"

She shook her head, her expression one of bitter disappointment. "That's the kind of stuff we deal with. Not usually every day, but still way too often. It ain't just 'bout the police. It's everywhere. We get looked at, talked down to, treated like we're less than human. You don't know what that's like, do you? To feel like you don't belong, like you're a suspect just 'cause the color of your skin."

Amara's eyes locked onto Robert's, her voice steady and resolute. "So when I see you sittin' here, bendin' the truth, tryin' to get this white defendant off, it's nuttin' new to me. Don't get it twisted — I see exactly what you're doin'. But you wouldn't be doing this if the defendant was a Black man. You've been bendin' the rules for far too long, and I'm tired of it. We all deserve justice, no matter the color of our skin."

Robert looked back at Amara, a wave of relief washing over him. She didn't know his secret. But mixed with that relief was a twinge of insult. The kind of cop she thought he was, the type she described, he didn't see himself that way.

He was a bit angry, and unsure of how to respond. His eyes wandered around the room. When they landed on Caroline, he saw her making the shape of a bridge with her hands, a silent reminder of their earlier conversation.

Robert realized then that Caroline brought out the good in him. Guilt overwhelmed him for not empathizing with the painful memories Amara had just shared and only thinking about himself. He reminded himself, 'Build the bridge.'

Looking at Amara, he said gently, "Do you have any family members who have stood trial and been found guilty?"

Amara's eyes narrowed slightly, but she answered quietly. "Yeah, I got two cousins servin' time. Both of 'em claimed they didn't do it, but it didn't matter. The system chewed 'em up and spit 'em out anyway."

Robert could feel the bridge being built. He said, "So you know personally the injustice of convicting an innocent man."

But she shook her head, her expression hardening. "No, despite their denials, they both guilty. But that don't mean justice was served. There's no justice for my cousins. They grew up poor, from a broken family. Their schools were more like trial prisons than places of learnin'. Ain't nothing like the schools in white neighborhoods."

Robert felt his unfinished bridge come crashing down before it could be completed, the weight of her words settling heavily on his shoulders.

Robert felt a surge of frustration and defeat wash over him. He had tried, but it seemed his efforts to connect with Amara had fallen flat. As he glanced over at Caroline, he saw her hands forming the shape of a bridge once again. Normally, such a gesture might have irritated him, but he noticed the serene expression on her face. It was a look of understanding and encouragement, as if she knew that building this bridge was difficult but worth the effort.

Her expression had a calming effect on him, instilling him with a renewed sense of determination and strength. With her silent support, Robert resolved to keep trying, to find common ground with Amara despite the challenges they faced. Then, an epiphone. Robert asked Amara if she had any children.

Amara's response was solemn as she mentioned her two boys, the eldest having just turned 16. She paused, surveying the room before continuing. "I bet some of you taught your kids how to drive," she began, her tone carrying a weight of significance. "Taught 'em the rules of right-of-way at all-way stops. Maybe taught 'em how to merge onto a highway. I just taught my 16-year-old how to drive. I told him that the most dangerous time in his life will be when he gets pulled over by a white cop."

There was a pause, a moment of silence that hung heavy in the air before she spoke again, her voice tinged with a mixture of sadness and resolve. "I bet none of you white folk had to teach your kids that," she added pointedly, her gaze settling on Robert. Her eyes held a piercing intensity, as if challenging him to acknowledge the reality of her words.

Despite her anger, Robert didn't see this as another failure. He pushed forward and seized the opportunity to further bridge the gap between them. "Have you ever thought about your child being wrongfully accused and put on trial?" he asked, his tone earnest.

Amara's response was immediate and resolute. "There isn't a Black parent anywhere that ain't worried their child will face injustice in the American system of justice," she replied, her voice carrying the weight of conviction. "It's one of the biggest fears I have for my boys."

Robert continued, his words deliberate. "And I imagine you wouldn't be too happy if there was a white woman on your son's jury who said that there's nothing anyone can say to change her guilty vote."

Amara's reaction was immediate, her expression frozen in shock as she recognized her own words mirrored back at her. Then, unexpectedly, tears began to well in her eyes, her strong facade crumbling before everyone's eyes.

It was a startling sight for the other jurors, who had become accustomed to Amara's outward strength and independence. Seeing her vulnerable and emotional left them silent, unsure of how to respond.

The silence was shattered by Caroline, her voice cutting through the tension. "A woman is crying and not a single gentleman in the room!" she exclaimed, her tone a mix of incredulity and reproach.

As if on cue, Blake approached Amara with a box of tissues in hand. His movements were deliberate yet gentle, his body language portraying humility and compassion. As he offered the tissues to her, his eyes conveyed a silent understanding, reflecting his willingness to provide support in a moment of vulnerability. It was a small gesture, but it spoke volumes about his newfound empathy and respect for his fellow juror.

Amara took a tissue but continued to cry softly, her emotions overwhelming her. Gradually, she began to nod her head in affirmation, her tears still flowing. The foreperson, recognizing the significance of her response, spoke up. "So, you're changing your vote?" he asked, his voice conveying both kindness and gentle insistence. Amara, still nodding, confirmed her decision with her continued gesture.

CHAPTER 12

Another Envelope!

Five weeks had passed since the trial ended, and life had ostensibly returned to normal for Robert. Each day unfolded with a comforting predictability. He woke up early, just as he always had, and started his day with a strong cup of coffee and the morning newspaper. Actually, it was a new brand of coffee – that was different. The coffee at the courthouse wasn't the greatest, but it gave him some ideas on a new blend. The ritual of reading the headlines, lingering over the sports section, and solving the crossword puzzle provided a sense of stability, a tether to the ordinary world.

His afternoons were filled with the familiar rhythms of retirement. He enjoyed long walks through the neighborhood with his dog, stopping occasionally to chat with neighbors or to admire the blooming flowers in their gardens. Those walks were always relaxing.

He resumed his volunteer work at the local library, where he sorted books and helped with community events. Robert always believed that giving back to your community was important. Evenings were spent in front of the television, watching his favorite crime dramas, or indulging in his newfound passion for cooking. The kitchen, once a place of necessity, had become a haven where he could experiment with recipes and savor the simple pleasures of a well-cooked meal. In retirement, money, in some sense, was replaced with time. And he enjoyed using some of that time to cook five star meals. Well, he thought they were five star.

Everything was as it should be, or so he tried to convince himself. Despite the comforting routines and the semblance of normalcy, a persistent unease lingered in the back of Robert's mind. He hadn't confessed during the deliberations, but there were moments when he wondered if it might have been better if he had. Each time he replayed the trial in his mind, a nagging sense of unfinished business ate away at him. It wasn't regret, but an unsettling feeling that something was still fundamentally wrong, a shadow that refused to lift no matter how much he tried to bury it beneath the trappings of ordinary life. Had he not accomplished a good deed? He helped make sure an innocent man was not convicted.

Fate seldom offers second chances for

redemption, yet for Robert fate seemed unusually determined not to be done with him just yet. As Robert stood in his kitchen, the savory scent of lunch wafting through the air, he remained unaware of fate's looming plans.

The kitchen was warm and inviting, filled with the rich aroma of simmering tomato sauce and freshly baked bread. Sunlight streamed through the window, casting a golden glow over the countertops cluttered with spices, utensils, and half-prepared ingredients. The radio played softly in the background, a mellow tune that seemed to blend seamlessly with the comforting sounds of bubbling pots and sizzling pans. Occasionally, Robert would even do a twirl or even almost dance.

Robert stirred the sauce absentmindedly, his thoughts wandering back to the trial, to the faces of the jurors, and to the weight of the secret he still carried. He had almost managed to convince himself that life could go on as usual, that he could lock away the past and forget the choices he had made. He had thought that would be possible after the trial. But something had eluded him.

Just as he reached for a spoon to taste his creation, the doorbell rang, its sharp sound cutting through the domestic tranquility like a knife. Robert paused, his heart skipping a beat. Visitors were rare, and something felt ominous, as if the universe were reminding him that some debts must be paid. He wiped his hands on a towel and made his way to the door. His gut was tightening, like in college right before an exam he hadn't studied for. Somehow, it felt to Robert that his past was about to catch up with him.

Opening the door, Robert found himself face-to-face with a courier who held a crisp, white envelope for him. Robert signed for the envelope, dread all over his face, and turned to close the door. He stopped for a moment, his thumbs rubbing up and down the name of the sender: Sheriff Hogan's Office. He momentarily contemplated whether there were any options to prevent mail from being delivered to his home. He felt like his life would be better without mail, or at least without any more crisp, white envelopes.

Robert's hands trembled slightly as he opened the letter. His eyes quickly scanned the contents:

"Dear Mr. Carter:

I hope this letter finds you well. I received your contact information from the Police Chief. I am sending you this letter to request a meeting with you for next week. I wish to discuss with you, as I have with most of the other jurors already, the trial for which you recently sat as a juror. The meeting is entirely voluntary and I have no questions, I just want to hear your thoughts about this matter.

I am available on Thursday at 2:30 PM or Friday at 8:30 AM. Further correspondence can be conducted by phone or email, as noted on this letterhead. I await your reply.

Godspeed,
Sheriff Hogan."

A sense of unease settled over Robert as he read the words. What could Sheriff Hogan possibly want to discuss about the trial now, weeks after its conclusion? He folded the letter carefully and placed it back in its envelope, his mind already racing with questions and apprehensions.

Robert thought about the letter for a few moments. Then he did the only thing he really felt that he could do. He sat down at his computer and typed an email to Sheriff Hogan, confirming he would be there for Thursday at 2:30 PM.

❖ ❖ ❖

Thursday had arrived. After being directed by the receptionist, Robert walked into Sheriff Hogan's office, taking in the familiar surroundings. The Sheriff stood up from behind his desk, extending a hand in greeting.

"Mr. Carter, good to see you," Sheriff Hogan said warmly.

"Likewise, Sheriff Hogan," Robert replied, shaking his hand firmly. "So, what's this about? Why send a letter about this meeting? Why not just call or shoot an email?"

Sheriff Hogan smiled, a hint of amusement in his eyes. "Well, Mr. Carter, to be frank, I wanted a written record of my request. Call me old-fashioned, but there's something about a letter that feels more official, more permanent. Plus, you never know when technology might fail us."

Robert nodded, understanding the Sheriff's reasoning. "Fair enough, Sheriff. So, what did you want to discuss?"

Sheriff Hogan settled back into his chair, his expression turning more serious. "Mr. Carter, I have to admit, I was surprised by how long the jury deliberated. I thought it would take no more than half a day, maybe just an hour or two, and you'd come back with a guilty verdict. But the not guilty verdict, well, it shook half the county."

Robert remained silent, his face unreadable.

"The victim's family," Sheriff Hogan continued, "they've asked me to look into the situation. They want to understand what happened in that jury room, why the decision went the way it did. They're devastated, Mr. Carter, and they're searching for answers. I need to know if there was anything unusual, any pressure or influence that might have affected the jury's decision."

Robert leaned forward. "Sheriff Hogan, isn't this the Police Chief's responsibility? They were the ones in charge of the investigation. Up to now, there hasn't been any involvement from the Sheriff's office."

Sheriff Hogan sighed, clasping his hands on the desk. "Everything in this county falls under my jurisdiction, Mr. Carter. You're right, though

— typically, this would be the Police Chief's responsibility. But the victim's family came to me directly. They trust me, and I felt a duty to them. Plus, with all due respect, the Chief's been swamped. And sometimes it takes a fresh set of eyes to see things clearly."

He paused, a thoughtful look on his face. "I did reach out to the Chief to make sure he was on board with what I'm doing, and he gave me the green light. I assure you, this isn't about stepping on toes. It's about finding the truth and bringing some peace to a grievin' family. As the Good Book says, 'Blessed are the peacemakers.'"

Sheriff Hogan reached over to his mouse, his expression turning confused as he fumbled with it. "Confounded technology," he muttered under his breath, shaking his head. After a moment, he seemed to find what he was looking for and clicked.

"I've just turned on the two cameras in my office," he informed Robert, motioning to one camera in each corner of the room. "It's standard procedure for these kinds of meetings. Do you have any objections to being recorded, Mr. Carter?"

Robert paused before answering, his eyes moving from one camera to the other as he took in the whole room. His police instinct made him absorb every detail. It was a typical sheriff's office: a sturdy wooden desk, shelves filled with law enforcement manuals, framed commendations, and a few family photos. His gaze fell on a cross hung on the wall with the Ten Commandments beside it.

The religious symbols were a testament to Sheriff Hogan's faith, subtly integrated into his professional space. Even though there wasn't an ashtray in sight, the air carried a pleasant mixture of coffee and cigars, with maybe a faint smell of bourbon.

Robert continued to survey the room for a moment before turning back to Sheriff Hogan. "I have no objection to being recorded," he said, his tone measured. "But what kind of meeting is this exactly?"

Sheriff Hogan leaned back in his chair, a jovial smile spreading across his face. "Oh, it's just a discussion, Mr. Carter. No formal questions, really. Just a friendly chat to go over a few things. And remember, you can leave anytime you want. No pressure."

"Would you like a cup o' Joe?" Sheriff Hogan asked, motioning towards a nook off of one side of the room.

Robert nodded, his eyes scanning the room as he followed the Sheriff's gesture. He tried to find where the Sheriff hid the cigars and bourbon, but it seemed that was going to remain a mystery.

His gaze settled on the makeshift, walk-in, coffee nook. It looked like the space was originally a remnant of a past era, though Robert wasn't quite sure what it once was. It was wider than a typical coat closet that a room like this might have, and too deep for one for sure. Robert decided that its past life was probably as a large supply closet, housing police forms, envelopes, and other paperwork, a relic of the pre-digital age. With the advent of technology, the need for such storage had dwindled. But now, it served a new purpose, catering to the Sheriff's apparent love for coffee, another thing they both seemed to share.

Robert poured himself a cup of coffee, settling into a relaxed demeanor around the Sheriff. Despite the ease of their interaction, he couldn't shake the familiarity of the Sheriff's tactics — a reminiscent strategy from his days as a detective, prying for crucial case details.

Resolved to enjoy the Sheriff's company without succumbing to his investigative intent, Robert posed the question, "So, what's on your mind, Sheriff?" Truth be told, he felt like saying, 'Bless me, Father, for I have sinned. It's been five years since I've been to confession.' Slightly amused with himself, he settled back into the chair in front of the Sheriff's desk, ready for whatever discussion lay ahead.

The Sheriff leaned back in his chair, his expression thoughtful as he mentioned his discussions with most of the jurors. Recounting snippets from their deliberations, he expressed his bewilderment at the drastic shift from a unanimous guilty verdict to a unanimous not guilty verdict. "In all my days, Mr. Carter, I've never seen such a turnaround," he remarked, shaking his head slightly. "Tell me anything you'd like about that."

Robert listened intently, his mind processing the Sheriff's words. Despite the casual tone of the conversation, the weight of the Sheriff's inquiry hung heavy in the air. Robert nodded, his expression thoughtful. "Absolutely, Sheriff. You see, a jury's duty is to go over the evidence with a fine-tooth comb. It's not about personal biases or gut feelings. It's about meticulously examining every piece of evidence presented, scrutinizing it from every angle, and weighing it against the facts of the case. And sometimes, as they do that, jurors uncover truths that weren't apparent at first glance."

The Sheriff nodded, his expression pensive. "I see."

In the midst of an awkward silence, Robert cautiously directed the conversation toward the deliberations, meticulously detailing the actions and viewpoints of his fellow jurors. Yet, amidst his thorough account, Robert conspicuously avoided discussing his own role in the deliberations. With a subtle finesse, he sidestepped any mention of his personal contributions, shrouding his involvement in secrecy.

The Sheriff nodded thoughtfully. "You know, Mr. Carter, listening to the accounts from your other jurors, I think there was more at play than what you're saying. The whole thing reminds me of the parable of the Good Samaritan."

Robert had a hint of curiosity in his expression. Robert was moderately religious, or at least he once was. But he couldn't understand the relevance here of the widely known story of the Good Samaritan. Robert's expression shifted to one of puzzlement. "How does that relate to the circumstances of the jury?" he inquired, genuinely intrigued.

The Sheriff sat up a little straighter, his expression grave yet earnest. "You know, the Good Samaritan parable is about this traveler who was attacked by robbers and left for dead on the road. A priest and a Levite passed by without helping. They assessed the situation and determined it was too risky for them. But a Samaritan stopped to aid the half-dead man, regardless of the risks."

"If it weren't for that one man, this traveler likely would have died," Sheriff Hogan added solemnly. "That parable reveals to good men that we must meet our moral and ethical responsibility to help someone in need, regardless of the potential cost or dangers to ourselves. The essence of God's law, and when we get it right, man's too, is not about rules but about mercy and compassion, regardless of our differences or prejudices."

As the Sheriff concluded his retelling of the parable, a weighted silence lingered in the room. Robert sensed the Sheriff's expectation, the subtle invitation for him to respond, but he remained resolute, opting instead to maintain his guarded stance.

Finally, breaking the silence, the Sheriff asserted, drawing from his interactions with other jurors, that there seemed to have been a 'Good Samaritan' among them, someone who, in his view, had gone out of his way and saved the defendant when none of the others would – at first.

Robert's expression shifted subtly, conveying a sense of confusion as he absorbed the Sheriff's insinuation. "I understand the meaning of the parable, Sheriff. What I don't understand is what you're trying to say exactly," he replied inquisitively, his tone tinged with a hint of curiosity and skepticism.

The Sheriff leaned back in his chair, his expression thoughtful yet composed. "Now, Mr. Carter, I'm not trying to say anything," he began, his voice carrying a measured cadence. "But it seems to me like you got something on your mind. Something you haven't quite put into words just yet."

Robert's gaze narrowed, a flicker of apprehension dancing behind his eyes. "I'm not sure I follow, Sheriff," he responded cautiously, his mind racing to discern the true intent behind the Sheriff's seemingly casual demeanor.

Sheriff Hogan leaned forward, his gaze steady as he quoted from the book of Proverbs. "He that covereth his sins shall not prosper: but whoso confesseth and forsaketh them shall have mercy."

The words resonated in the room, their solemnity underscoring the gravity of confession in matters of justice and redemption. With a quiet intensity, the Sheriff emphasized the timeless wisdom of scripture, emphasizing how confession is good for the confessor.

As the biblical passage hung in the air, Sheriff Hogan's expression remained unchanged, his conviction unwavering. In his eyes, confession was not merely a legal obligation but a spiritual imperative, a pathway to absolution and grace.

For Robert, the weight of the Sheriff's words was palpable, their resonance stirring something deep within him. At that moment, he couldn't help but reflect on the significance of confession, its power to heal and redeem, even in the face of darkness and uncertainty.

Sheriff Hogan's voice carried a somber tone as he leaned back in his chair, his gaze drifting momentarily to the clutter of papers on his desk. "You know, Mr. Carter," he began, his words measured and reflective, "most of the cases I've worked on were resolved not because of the strength of the evidence, but because of the suspect's desire to confess."

He paused, his expression pensive, before continuing. "Sure, there were times when the evidence was overwhelming, undeniable even. But for some, it was their deep sense of regret that led them to confess. The burden of their actions became too much to bear, and confession offered them a release, a chance at redemption."

The Sheriff's words hung in the air, yet they were also heavy with the weight of his years in law enforcement. In his eyes, confession wasn't just a legal strategy — it was a profound human response to the moral complexities of wrongdoing and accountability.

Robert's demeanor shifted slightly as he

absorbed the Sheriff's words, his expression reflecting a mix of contemplation and defiance. After a moment of reflection, he responded, his voice steady but tinged with a hint of defiance. "I don't feel any regret," he stated firmly, his gaze meeting the Sheriff's with unwavering resolve.

Despite the weight of the Sheriff's words and the implications they carried, Robert remained steadfast in his assertion. There was a steely resolve in his tone, a conviction that echoed through the quiet of the office.

To be clear, though, Robert did feel guilt. When the memory of the shots fired, each recoil of the Smith & Wesson, replayed in his mind he always felt guilt. He'd known others in law enforcement who had to kill someone and they felt guilty about it too, even when their actions were 100% justified. Killing another human being is not an easy thing for most people to do, despite what you might see in the movies.

But when Robert peeled back that layer of guilt, there was no regret. His upbringing, his values, all screamed at him that what he did was wrong. But also knew that he'd do it again if given the opportunity.

"And yet you have this desire to confess," the Sheriff remarked, his tone softening with a touch of compassion.

Robert fell into a contemplative silence, the weight of the Sheriff's observation settling heavily upon him. It was a stark truth laid bare, one that resonated deeply within him. As the silence stretched on, it seemed almost natural, as if anyone observing could discern the profound introspection taking place.

It was undeniable — there was a part of him that yearned to unburden himself, to confess the truth that weighed heavily upon his soul. He couldn't shake the feeling that his inadvertent slip-ups during the deliberations were the workings of his subconscious, nudging him toward confession.

At that moment, Robert couldn't deny it any longer. The Sheriff's words had struck a chord, revealing a truth he could no longer ignore. Despite his resistance, despite the risks involved, he harbored a deep-seated desire to confess. But that did not mean that confession was the right thing to do.

Robert glanced up at the two cameras perched in the corners of the room, their lenses capturing every detail. His gaze then drifted toward the coffee nook, a subtle diversion from the weighty conversation at hand. With a faint smile, he turned back to the Sheriff.

"You know, Sheriff, my sweet tooth seems to have gained a bit more sway over my desires as I've gotten older," Robert remarked casually, a hint of levity in his tone. "Mind if I add another cube or two of sugar to my coffee?"

To a less experienced observer, Robert's seemingly casual request for more sugar might have appeared as a deliberate attempt to sidestep an impending confession. Yet, Sheriff Hogan, with his years of experience, seemed to understand the weight of the moment and simply nodded in acknowledgment.

Robert made his way to the corner of the coffee nook where the sugar was kept. Though the distance wasn't great, every step felt like an eternity as his mind grappled with the decision he was about to make. As he reached for the sugar, a fleeting thought brought a wistful smile to his lips.

"Sugar," he murmured to himself, recalling Caroline's endearing Southern accent. He often found himself reflecting on her perspective, wondering what she would advise. Would she advocate for honesty and accountability in this moment, even at the cost of personal sacrifice? Robert couldn't help but believe she would, and she'd somehow give him the strength to do it. He drew some strength from that thought.

Robert leaned against a corner in the coffee nook, his grip tightening around the warm mug as he took a tentative sip. In the quiet of the room, he half-hoped that Sheriff Hogan would break the silence, perhaps offering some unexpected intervention that might steer him away from his impending confession. Yet, deep down, Robert knew such a reprieve was unlikely to materialize.

As the silence stretched between them, Robert shifted uncomfortably, his eyes darting around the room. "What if I just … walk out?" he ventured, his voice betraying a hint of uncertainty.

Sheriff Hogan's response was immediate, his tone firm but not unkind. "I wouldn't appreciate that, Mr. Carter," he stated, his gaze unwavering. "I think you've got somethin' to say that I want to hear." Robert knew full well that the Sheriff knew he wasn't about to leave.

Robert's gaze drifted down to something poking out from the Sheriff's coat — a telltale shape that caught his professional eye in the courtroom. With a subtle gesture, he indicated the object. His expression conveyed a sense of curiosity as well as recognition, prompting the Sheriff to glance down to where the gun peeked out from beneath his coat.

With a faint smile, he reached for the weapon, gently pulling back the coat that had been concealing it. "This here's my S&W revolver," he explained, his voice tinged with a touch of nostalgia. "Was my daddy's. It's an old Smith & Wesson Model 10, .38 Special. Been in the family for years. My daddy carried it on the force back in the day. It's got a six-round cylinder and a 4-inch barrel. It's got character, history. It's no fancy Glock, but it's a favorite among those in law enforcement. And it can kill a man just as easily," Sheriff Hogan stated solemnly, meeting Robert's gaze with a firm resolve.

Robert understood what the Sheriff was saying. Finally, after a moment of contemplation, Robert straightened up, his gaze meeting the Sheriff's expectant eyes. "Okay, Sheriff," he began, his voice steady but tinged with apprehension, still leaning into the corner, less for physical support, it would seem, than moral. "Truthfully, I'm scared. But I think, finally, I now have to give a confession."

CHAPTER 13

Confession is Necessary for Good People

Robert began his confession with a weighty declaration. "Everyone was surprised by our acquittal," he said, his voice measured and resolute. "The truth is that everyone was right that there was one guilty man in that courtroom. It just wasn't the one everyone had suspected." As he spoke, the gravity of his words hung in the air, punctuating the tension that filled the room.

Robert asked, "Do you have a family, Sheriff?"

Sheriff Hogan paused for a moment, a soft smile spreading across his face. "Yes, Mr. Carter, I do. My wife's name is Mary. We've been together for twenty-five years now. We met in college, at a small-town dance in Kentucky." Family was a topic the Sheriff obviously held close to his heart.

He continued, his voice warming with affection as he spoke of his children. "We have four kids. Our oldest, Daniel, is twenty-three. He's just finished law school and is about to start his first job as a public defender. Next is Michael, he's twenty-one and studying engineering. Then there's Sam, he's nineteen and still in high school, trying to figure out if he wants to follow his older brother's footsteps, mine, or carve his own path. And finally, there's little Tommy, he's just thirteen and full of energy. He's always getting into something, keeping us on our toes."

As he spoke, it was clear that Sheriff Hogan was deeply proud of his family, each word laced with love and fondness. Robert listened, his face softening as the Sheriff described his family. When the Sheriff finished, Robert looked down for a moment, as if searching for the right words. "I was married," he said quietly, "but she died four years ago."

He paused, swallowing hard and collecting himself. "We couldn't have any children … she couldn't have any children." The admission seemed to drain the color from his face, and he felt literally weak in the knees, as if the weight of his words was too much to bear.

"May I sit down again, Sheriff?" Robert asked, his voice barely above a whisper.

"Of course, Mr. Carter," the Sheriff replied gently.

Robert lowered himself back into the chair,

his movements slow and deliberate. As he sat, his eyes were drawn to a framed family photo on the Sheriff's desk. It seemed to be a recent photo. It showed Sheriff Hogan, his wife Mary, and their four boys, all beaming with happiness. The image of a family so full of life and love contrasted starkly with the emptiness Robert felt inside, deepening the ache in his heart.

Robert looked up at the Sheriff, his eyes clouded with a mix of emotions. "Sheriff, I'm not avoiding my confession. This is my confession."

Sheriff Hogan's expression remained compassionate, urging Robert to continue.

"My wife didn't just die four years ago. She committed suicide," Robert's voice broke as he spoke the last word, his hand instinctively raised to cover his mouth. His breathing grew heavier, each inhale and exhale a struggle against the weight of his feelings.

Robert's gaze shifted to the cross hanging on the wall, maybe seeking solace in its presence. He wanted to feel anger, to lash out at the unfairness of it all, but the anger wouldn't come. Instead, a profound sorrow settled over him. No, that wasn't it either. Even after all these years, Robert was still confused by his emotions. What did he feel? He felt failure, that's for sure. A deep, all-consuming sense of failure.

As the silence stretched on, Robert finally spoke again, his voice barely a whisper. "I couldn't save her, Sheriff. I failed her in every way that mattered."

The Sheriff stood up and walked over to an antique filing cabinet, his back turned to Robert. At first, the stop seemed normal, just a moment to gather his thoughts, but as the seconds stretched into an uncomfortable silence, Robert realized something wasn't right. Why had he stopped there for so long?

Finally, after a long period of reflection, the Sheriff spoke, his voice slightly muffled, words thick with emotion as they filtered through the barrier of his back. "I haven't been fully truthful with you."

Another long pause hung in the air, the weight of unspoken words pressing down on both men. There seemed to have been a bond developed between these two. Then he continued, his voice carrying a sorrowful resonance. "I had five children. She would have been sixteen this very day. Sweet sixteen."

The Sheriff reached for a baseball on the top of the cabinet, its surface seeming like new, unworn or faded. He turned and walked back to Robert, his steps heavy with the burden of memory. Handing the baseball to Robert, he let the silence between them speak of shared grief and unspoken understanding.

"We went to see a ball game on a trip to New York. Bottom of the ninth, bases loaded, Yankees down by three. She catches that fly ball that won the game for the Yankees. She was a Yankee fan every day after that." He paused, a faint smile touching his lips before it faded. "I hate the Yankees."

"Every day," he scoffed. "She died two months later. She was run over by a drunk driver while she was riding her bike. A driver I chose to let off with a warning only weeks earlier. Billy. Good ol' Billy. He pleaded with me, said he'd lose his job. Everyone knew his wife was getting cancer treatment that Billy could barely afford. What was I supposed to do?" The Sheriff's voice trembled with emotion. "Oh heck, I know what I was supposed to do. I was supposed to do my job. So, Mr. Carter, I'm a failure too, it would seem."

The Sheriff returned to his seat behind his desk, the weight of his words lingering in the air. His face, etched with lines of sorrow and regret, betrayed the heavy burden he carried. "I feel like such a failure that I can't put up pictures of her in my office because I can't bear her looking at me." There was an awkward silence. "So there's pictures in drawers and there's mementos of her throughout the office, like that ball."

Robert, with genuine concern in his voice, kindly asked, "Did you ever confess?"

The Sheriff sighed deeply, his eyes filled with a mixture of sadness and guilt. "Not at first. How could I tell my wife that I'm the reason our little girl is dead?" His voice trembled, and his expression grew even more pained as he continued. "It drove us apart. Nearly ended our marriage. Robert, one day I literally dropped to my knees and begged her for forgiveness. I wept like a baby." The Sheriff's face contorted with the anguish of the memory, his eyes glistening with unshed tears. "She had no idea what was going on because even if she could make out the words amidst my mumbling and sobbing, I don't think I was making any sense. It was too much, Robert. Finally, I managed to put together a coherent sentence and tell her what I had done." Robert somehow understood that he was the first person the Sheriff had mentioned this too outside of his family.

The Sheriff paused, his eyes distant and filled with a deep-seated pain. "The day I confessed to her was the second worst day of my life."

Robert asked with a sense of bewilderment, "So you're saying confession is bad?"

The Sheriff shook his head, his expression somber. He shifted his weight forward, as if to compose himself, and said, "No, I'm saying it's hard. Damn hard. And risky, too. And the bigger the sin, the riskier and harder it is." His voice was firm but compassionate. "Confession is necessary for good people. For the wicked, well, they don't believe redemption is possible. But for righteous folk like us, Robert, it's required to heal our souls which allows us to move forward with our lives." Robert let all of this sink in. He had already committed to confessing, and he probably knew for a long time now that he needed to. He didn't need to hear the Sheriff's words. But it helped.

Robert allowed the Sheriff's words to settle within him. He had wrestled with the weight of his secret for what felt like an eternity, knowing deep down that he needed to unburden himself of the truth. The Sheriff's words reinforced what Robert had long suspected but perhaps had been too afraid to acknowledge.

As the Sheriff spoke, Robert felt a subtle shift within himself, a loosening of the tightly wound coil of guilt and fear that had gripped his heart for so long. He had already made his decision, but hearing the Sheriff's words gave him a sense of validation.

The Sheriff opened a drawer in the desk, the creak of wood breaking the silence that hung in the air. He pulled out a picture of his daughter and quietly placed it on his desk as a faint smile appeared on his face.

Very quickly, in a monotone voice, Robert said, "I killed him." Then, at a slightly slower pace, looking down at the floor, he said again, "I killed him."

CHAPTER 14

The Details

Robert took a deep breath, the weight of his words pressing heavily on his chest as he looked at the Sheriff. "The victim, Andrew Johnson, molested and raped my wife when she was four years old and he was 18. Her parents tried to file a complaint, but they were poor, and the Johnsons were rich and well-connected. They immediately sent their son overseas, moving him from country to country until things settled down. Mary's parents went to the police many times, but the police didn't even open a file."

He paused, gathering his thoughts before continuing. "I loved my wife dearly, but it wasn't all good times. She never faced and resolved her issues. She couldn't have children because of what happened. It all weighed on her. She tried to commit suicide once before. I got her help, and although things weren't perfect, I actually thought they were basically fine. I was wrong." Robert paused. "It was the anniversary of when it happened, and three weeks before her fortieth birthday. She left a note. It had four words: 'There must be justice.'

The police asked me what it meant, and I told them I wasn't sure, that it must have something to do with my job. But I knew my wife; I knew what those words meant – there was no doubt in my mind. She wanted me to kill Johnson."

Robert's voice quivered slightly, but his resolve was clear. "For six months, I was consumed by grief, and layered on top of that was my wife's final request, a request I wasn't sure I was capable of fulfilling. After six months, I decided to do some research. If I could find evidence that Johnson was still hurting children – people – then maybe I could muster the courage to fulfill my wife's last request. I searched the internet, used my access to police records, but after six months of looking I found nothing.

Then I turned fifty-five and I was eligible for early retirement. I retired and moved here. I decided I'd follow Johnson for one year, and if I didn't find anything, I'd move on. After a year, I didn't find anything. But I still couldn't move on."

Robert's eyes glistened with unshed tears as he continued, his voice steady but laden with emotion. "That dreadful night, I decided to confront Johnson. I told him who I was and what he did to my wife."

As Robert spoke, the Sheriff's face remained impassive, though a flicker of understanding and sympathy passed through his eyes. He leaned forward slightly, hands clasped together on the desk, listening intently. He didn't interrupt, didn't intervene; he wanted Robert to finish his confession. He could see the determination in Robert's eyes, the desperate need to unburden his soul.

Robert, his emotions raw but his resolve unwavering, waited for the Sheriff's reaction, feeling the weight of his words hanging heavily in the room. The Sheriff's silence spoke volumes, offering Robert the space to continue his painful story.

Robert took a deep breath, his voice trembling as he continued his confession. "Johnson smiled and said, 'I remember your wife.' He said he learned a valuable lesson after that. He remembered his parents moving him from country to country. He was surprised to learn that some countries turned a blind eye to what he was doing to children. Now he takes a trip to countries like that once per year, sometimes twice."

Robert paused, the memory clearly causing him distress. "That led to shouts and accusations, and then, without any warning, Johnson lunged at me. Things were so slippery I could barely stay standing. But my police training kicked in, and I redirected him, using his weight against him. Johnson couldn't remain standing and fell to the ground with a thud. It was a moment of risk for me, that's for sure. But I regained my composure and I could have safely stepped back. But I didn't. I shot him. Twice."

The sight of Johnson's lifeless body sprawled on the driveway was unlike anything Robert had ever experienced. As a former detective, he'd seen his fair share of dead bodies, but this one was different. This wasn't a crime scene he had stumbled upon; this was a dead body he had created. Johnson lay motionless, his eyes open but unseeing, a pool of blood slowly spreading around him.

The two bullet wounds were stark and final, the pool of blood was flowing slowly down the driveway. Robert remembered feeling a strange detachment, yet his heart pounded in his chest. He had shot at people before, but always in the line of duty, always with a purpose to protect. This was cold and calculated. His actions weighed heavily on him. The finality of death was no longer an abstract concept after that; it had been right there in front of him, a testament to the lengths he had gone to for vengeance.

His voice broke slightly, but he pressed on, determined to get it all out. "It wasn't self-defense. I did what I had come to do, if necessary. After that, I adjusted the crime scene. I made sure there wasn't anything to incriminate me, or at least so I thought, and I left some clues that would redirect the police. For example, I took out Johnson's wallet and grabbed the cash to make it seem like this was a robbery gone wrong."

The Sheriff listened intently, his face a mask of contemplation and concern. His eyes revealed a deep understanding, tinged with sadness, but he remained silent, letting Robert finish his confession. The room felt heavy with the weight of Robert's words, the air thickened by his admission.

Robert recounted how he went home that night, removed the plastic coverings in the car and burnt it along with everything he was wearing. Then he calmly disassembled his Smith & Wesson, meticulously wiping down each part and filing off the serial number and other identifiable marks.

He placed the parts into a heavy-duty polypropylene container filled with hydrochloric acid. He left the parts submerged for several hours to ensure any biological traces were completely eradicated. This also served to corrode the barrel's rifling enough to prevent bullet matching.

After the parts had soaked, he carefully retrieved the pieces with special tongs and acid-resistant gloves, neutralized them in a baking soda solution, and washed them down. To further ensure the barrel could not be matched to the bullets, he used a metal rod to scrape the inside, obliterating any remaining rifling marks. He then damaged key parts like the barrel and firing pin, ensuring they could never be used again. Each piece was then placed into a small, heavy-duty plastic bag, and sealed shut.

"The parts of that gun are buried in all four corners of the tri-county area," Robert said, his voice steady, almost mechanical.

The Sheriff absorbed the full weight of Robert's confession, his eyes flickering with a mix of emotions — understanding, sorrow, and the heavy burden of knowing. The room was thick with tension, each word Robert spoke hanging in the air like a tangible presence.

Having unburdened his soul, Robert looked directly at the Sheriff, waiting for his reaction. The Sheriff's face remained inscrutable, a reflection of the complexity of the situation and the shared pain of their respective confessions.

The Sheriff took a moment, then asked softly, "How do you feel, Robert?"

Robert paused, he searched for the right words, the right way to describe the newfound sense of freedom coursing through him. Finally, he looked up and replied with quiet certainty, "Light."

The Sheriff nodded, understanding the profound simplicity of that single word. The room seemed to contrast Robert's newfound feeling, calm but heavy with the echoes of Robert's confession.

But the Sheriff knew he now had to break that calm. He leaned forward, his voice grave. "You know what I have to do now, right?"

Robert leaned forward in turn and looked at him, the weight of reality settling back in. With a faint, bitter smile, he asked, "Let me go?"

CHAPTER 15

Check and Mate

The Sheriff shook his head, his expression firm. "There are consequences to our actions, Mr. Carter. The law must reign supreme. It is my duty to arrest you. Sure, there's a part of me that wants to let you go, but after Billy, I've learned all too well never to listen to that part of me again."

Robert's eyes narrowed. "On what basis are you planning on making this arrest?"

The Sheriff blinked, momentarily dumbfounded by the question. "Based on the confession you just made, Mr. Carter."

"But you never read me my Miranda rights, Sheriff," Robert retorted.

The Sheriff had been preparing to get out of his seat, but with Robert's response, he settled back into his chair. A look of disappointment crossed his face. "Mr. Carter, this was never an interrogation. Not with you and not with any of the other former jurors. I never had to read you your Miranda rights. I never asked you any questions; you volunteered everything. I think the only question I put to you was if you wanted a cup of coffee. Come on, Mr. Carter, you know better. You freely gave a spontaneous confession, and that can be used against you, with or without Miranda rights. You were always free to leave. You know how this works; you were in law enforcement."

Robert's gaze was steady as he replied, "I think you should play back your video, Sheriff Hogan, because that's not at all what happened. You told me I couldn't leave and threatened me with your gun if I didn't confess."

The Sheriff's hand hovered over the mouse, his irritation palpable. With a begrudging sigh, he grabbed the mouse, his fingers tapping against the surface as he rewound the footage to just before Robert's confession. Pausing the video, he leaned closer to the screen, his brow furrowing in surprise.

Glancing around the room, he noticed the cameras stationed in each corner. His gaze shifted to the coffee nook, a realization dawning upon him. "Well, I'll be," he muttered to himself. "When I converted that supply closet to a coffee nook, I never considered the cameras. Who needs to record what's going on in a closet?" The Sheriff had just come to the realization that the cameras didn't record any video from where Robert had been in the coffee nook.

Robert watched the Sheriff's reaction, his expression unreadable. "It doesn't matter that there's no video of me since your cameras can't capture anything in the location I was standing," Robert interjected. "Let's play it and listen to the audio. It won't have any problem capturing audio."

The Sheriff hit play, waiting in wonder to what he might actually hear.

What if I just … walk out?

I wouldn't appreciate that, Mr. Carter. I think you've got something to say that I want to hear. This here's my S&W revolver. Was my daddy's. It's an old Smith & Wesson Model 10, .38 Special. Been in the family for years. My daddy carried it on the force back in the day. It's got a six-round cylinder and a 4-inch barrel. It's got character, history. It's no fancy Glock, but it's a favorite among those in law enforcement. And it can kill a man just as easily.

Okay, Sheriff. Truthfully, I'm scared. But I think, finally, I now have to give a confession.

Robert, with a satisfied smirk, said, "See, I couldn't leave and you threatened me with your gun. I was scared."

The Sheriff's response, "Well, I'll be," was

laced with a mix of surprise and admiration. He allowed a moment of silence to hang in the air, letting the implications of Robert's deception sink in. The room seemed to hold its breath, the meaning of the revelation settling over the two of them, or at least the Sheriff. The Sheriff seemed like a man not easily impressed. He took a deep breath and slowly exhaled, his eyes never leaving Robert's.

With a hint of wry amusement, he remarked, "You could outwit Daniel himself." His voice carried a grudging respect, acknowledging the cunning and resourcefulness Robert had demonstrated. The Sheriff leaned back in his chair, crossing his arms as he regarded Robert with a newfound curiosity.

"I've seen a lot in my time, but this … this takes the cake," he continued, shaking his head slightly. "Never thought I'd see the day when someone pulled the wool over my eyes like that."

Robert asked with a hint of hesitation, "So, we're done?"

The Sheriff responded with a succinct, "We're done."

What else could the Sheriff say? He didn't have any evidence to hold Robert, let alone charge him. The only thing linking him to the crime was his confession, and the Sheriff couldn't use that. The Sheriff might be relieved that he could let Robert go, but this was no act of charity. It was the only answer he could provide. The only thing this video could be used for now would be to show how the Sheriff was outwitted, not something that a man like Sheriff Hogan would appreciate anyone finding out about.

Robert then extended his hand for a shake, ready to depart. As they firmly shook hands the Sheriff's sudden shift in demeanor caught him off guard. "Oh, Robert, one more thing," the Sheriff said. He reached into his drawer and then held a crisp, white envelope for him.

Robert's initial impulse was to burn the envelope, not wanting to deal with any more unexpected surprises from crisp, white envelopes. The Sheriff then explained, "That Southern Belle gave it to me when I met with her."

With a mixture of curiosity and reluctance, Robert opened the envelope. As he examined its contents, the Sheriff elaborated, "She said it's her WhatsApp number? Do you even know how to use WhatsApp?"

Robert couldn't help but chuckle at the unexpected but cherished communication. "I don't have a clue," he admitted, "But I promise you, Sheriff, I'm going to figure it out."

ABOUT THE AUTHOR

Derik Brandt

Derik Brandt is an emerging author, poet, politician, senior executive, consultant, and occasional poker player. Born and raised in Sault Ste. Marie, a small city blessed with amazing outdoor experiences, Derik's hometown has profoundly influenced who he is. He earned a B.A. from Western University with a double major in Economics and Political Science. He also completed the Marketing Management Program at Columbia Business School, Columbia University, and earned a Masters Certificate in Municipal Leadership from the Schulich School of Business.

"Thank you for taking the time to read my book. I hope it entertained you and captivated you. If you enjoyed it, please give it a five star review online - it helps a great deal."

Manufactured by Amazon.ca
Acheson, AB